A Fl
Vampires

Everlyn C Thompson

DEDICATION

This one's for Fish.

A Flock of Vampires:
Bloddrikker Wars

CHAPTER 1

The wine was chilled to the perfect temperature. The music was kept low enough to encourage intimate conversation; and the lighting was dimmed, giving couples the illusion of privacy. Candlelight flickered and danced in the air each time the waitress passed by. The delicious smells that wafted from her tray made the breadsticks in the basket on the table taste like cardboard toilet-paper rolls.

But none of those things mattered if you were seated with someone at a table for two. Maybe one would only notice such things when seated alone. Either way, Keltti Callinwood had had plenty of time to observe the room.

With her hands, she nervously smoothed out her new dress. The royal blue bodice that hugged her chest flatteringly gave way to a full skirt, which had been a carefully budgeted splurge from a local dress-shop's discount rack. It was hard for her to hold still when she had tried it on; she loved the way it swayed around her calves when she moved.

She checked her phone again. Still no word. Her date should have been there thirty minutes ago. Letting out the breath that she'd been holding in, she waved the waitress over.

"Can I get the bill please?"

"The table is yours for another half an hour; are you sure you don't want to wait a little longer?" The waitress sounded optimistic, but Keltti could hear the thin layer of pity underneath.

"No, thanks. Just the bill."

The waitress nodded and headed toward the hostess stand at the front of the restaurant.

From the corner of her eye, Keltti saw a few heads turn in her direction, but she didn't bother to meet their gaze. She tipped back her wineglass for the last sip of her cabernet sauvignon as the waitress subtly slipped the billfold on the table.

After leaving money and a fair-sized tip for the wine, she had just a short walk through the busy restaurant. "Thanks," she murmured to the hostess, and she finally found herself standing on the sidewalk outside, staring up at the dark sky. There wasn't a star in view—downtown Calgary was one of the last places that you would likely see one.

Well, that was a total waste of time.

Her first attempt at dating in ten years and it had gone right down the toilet.

I suppose it could have been worse... If he had shown up and we had both gotten food poisoning from the food...

And if she was going to be totally honest with herself, it's possible that she was even a bit relieved at being stood up.

No awkward small talk, trying to get to know each other in a room full of strangers. No pressure at the end of the date for a good night kiss, wondering what he wants ... No, it was much easier this way.

Someone was going to get a big fucking stake in the heart tonight.

At this point, anyone would do. Any Goddamn thing that moved.

Stu crouched low, covered by the shadows of a dumpster in a dark alley in downtown Calgary. Somewhere ahead, three members of the Sterken (aka Rebels), a group of Vampires hell-bent on overthrowing the current Vampire King, were waiting for him. Behind him, two of his own soldiers waited, watching for their chance to take the Rebels out, while continuing to cover Stu's back.

It was still early for a Friday night—only a matter of time until an unsuspecting human stumbled into the middle of their standoff. The Rebel Vamps had no problem letting this little fight go public. Stu needed to end this soon. Like, five fucking minutes ago, soon. Or last week soon.

He raised his hand to signal that he was going in, and that Rostell and Arvid should cover his ass. Without looking back to make sure they were onboard with the plan, he jumped to his feet and unleashed a round of bullets in the Rebels' direction. Filled with a toxic combination of mercury and polonium, the bullets were lethal to both Immortals and humans alike.

An unhuman shriek echoed down the alley when one of Stu's bullets found its target. It didn't matter where the poisoned bullet had lodged itself. As long as it stayed in the Rebel's body, it would only be a matter of minutes before the Vamp kicked it. Too fucking humane in Stu's opinion— let the mo-fos suffer a little longer.

He crouched lower to peer around the corner of the next building, but he was quickly met with a hail of metal bullets.

Oh yeah—it was going to be a good night, he thought with a feral grin.

The cool evening breeze tugged at Keltti's upswept hair and tangled her dress around her legs.

Should have brought a coat, she thought to herself. Living next to the mountains could bring any kind of weather this time of year.

Walking downtown this late at night wasn't the smartest idea; anyone out looking for trouble would see a young woman alone and vulnerable. A chill crept down her back, leaving goose bumps in its wake. Something in the air didn't feel right. Even an untrained Witch such as Keltti could sense when something was off.

She had forsaken her more functional, everyday purse in the name of fashion, and the smaller one she carried tonight had nothing but her cell phone, a small amount of cash, her ID, and some lip gloss. Walking home alone in the dark hadn't been in her plans, and now she was missing the can of pepper spray she usually carried with her. A girl in the city could never be too careful.

Most Witches preferred to live in covens; sometimes, in a less traditional setting, small groups would share a house. But Keltti lived alone. Her close-knit sense of family, the sense, that bonded most Witches, had dried up after her mother's death. Grief and sadness had taken a harsh toll on everyone, and their pity towards Keltti had been the final straw that she couldn't bear to carry. She'd left, thirteen years ago, and had never gone back.

Her inheritance money was used to purchase a small two-bedroom bungalow in an older neighborhood. With a few repairs and upgrades, and a lot of TLC, it was now welcoming and cheerful, and boasted a large garden that took up most of the back yard. Most of the surrounding properties had fallen into disrepair, and were bought by large investment companies who tore them down and built up new, modern, three-story duplexes with postage stamp sized yards.

Only a couple more blocks to go. The river came into view, just past the homeless shelter.

Some yoga pants, a warm sweater and a hot cup of tea would be—

Keltti screamed as something huge and black flew out the alley and tackled her to the ground.

Oh Goddess, I've been hit by a truck—

The cement around her exploded into tiny shards that whipped up and hit her in the face. The not-so-distant sound of *pop, pop, pop,* made her realize that someone was shooting at her. She tried to scramble to her feet but found herself already being lifted into the air and manhandled into the nearest doorway.

A heavy hand pulled her backwards against a hard body that moved too fast to be human. A quick glance over her shoulders confirmed it was a Vampire—but not one of the nice safe civilian Vampires. No, his size and speed made him easy to identify as one of the King's Warriors. Her hands shot up to protect her neck, but he didn't seem to have an interest in biting her. Instead, he pushed her behind him and pulled out two handguns from underneath his long black coat.

"Stay down!" he shouted, not even bothering to look back at her.

She covered her head and burrowed even further back into the little nook behind him. The sound of gunfire filled the air again as he kept firing down the alley he had come from. If Keltti had been a shadow Witch, she could have protected herself with a defensive spell; possibly even an offensive one. But she had only minor healing skills, and for the hundredth time, she was wishing that she had decided to pursue an apprenticeship—but that was something to contemplate once she was safe in her bed, not when she was in the middle of an old-west style shoot out.

The glass window above Keltti exploded with a soft *ping,* and razor-sharp shards of glass rained down on her. Something hot and wet ran down her back, and her neck started to sting. The vampire turned back and pierced her with his dark eyes; saying without words that he knew she was bleeding.

This is what being prey feels like…

Just when she thought he'd never look away, he turned and shot at someone who had taken advantage of his distraction. A body fell to the cold pavement mere feet from where she was trapped.

He turned back to her, his gaze roving over her from head to toe, while he holstered his guns and reached for something electronic attached to his ear.

"One down. All clear. Status?" He continued to stare at her, and Keltti resisted the urge to squirm under his intense gaze.

"What? *Fuck!* Where—How bad is it?" Without waiting for an answer from whoever was on the other side of his earpiece, he took off running into the alley where he'd come flying out of minutes before. His long black coat flapped behind him, looking like a separate entity that was hesitant to follow.

Someone's hurt... Without any further thought, Keltti took off after him.

Stu rounded the corner at a top speed. Arvid lay in the middle of the alley, most of his chest covered in blood. He was still breathing—for now.

"Shit," Stu breathed, fear filling his veins with ice for the first time in weeks. "What happened?"

Rostell looked up from where he kneeled next to the bleeding Warrior. "Shot to the chest. Bullet's still in there."

Fuck. Fuck! Vampires could heal most wounds, but not with a bullet still inside. The Rebels' bullets were made to cause maximum damage. They contained a poison similar to what the King's Army used, which was toxic to Vampires. They had only minutes to get the bullet out before the tainted blood would kill Arvid.

Before he could call for an evac unit, a figure slipped past him and dropped to its knees next to the wounded soldier. It was the Witch that he'd saved earlier; he'd forgotten all about her when he had heard Ros on the comm link. With a growl, he grabbed her arm and hauled her away from the injured Vampire. She yelped in protest as Stu stepped between Arvid and her, completely blocking her view.

He could still smell the blood running down her back. She must be daft to have approached a wounded Vampire.

His fangs throbbed from the sweet smell; what the hell had she been thinking?

Holding her arm where he'd grabbed her, she stepped towards the fallen soldier again.

"He's hurt. I can help." He moved to intercept her again, but hesitated.

What the fuck... He never hesitated. Maybe he'd hit his head and hadn't realized it yet.

She held her hands up in a sign of surrender. "Let me help. Please." Her voice shook, and her eyes were wide with fear.

A quick glance and Stu knew Arvid didn't have time for the evac which he still hadn't called for. He was out of options, and they both knew it.

"Do it." He stepped aside, but followed close behind the small Witch as she lowered herself to Arvid's side. No way was he letting anyone close enough to hurt a fellow soldier; he would watch Arvid's back.

Keltti took a deep breath and placed both hands on the punctured chest in front of her.

She closed her eyes and looked inward to the place where her powers as a Witch came from. It took a few breaths for her to calm herself enough to find it. Slowly, she reached for the bright strands of light that made up the very center of her. Grasping one, she tugged until it came loose.

Now came the hardest part—extending it to her patient. The rope of light wanted to stay with her, like a sticky piece of spaghetti. It took multiple tries to direct it where she wanted it to go.

Finally, she was able to connect it to the injured Vampire. She felt a bead of sweat run down her neck, stinging when it found her abrasions.

She thrust her way through the outer layers of skin, bone, and muscle until she found the bullet. The tissue around it was rotting, poisoned by whatever was leaking from the bullet. Wrapping warm layers of healing light around it, she gently tugged. At first, the muscles resisted, but after her tender encouragement, they started to push the bullet out of the Vampire's body.

He hadn't taken a clean hit; the bullet had ricocheted off his ribs and bounced around before becoming lodged above his diaphragm. She needed to get it out as quickly as possible; the poison was rapidly leaching into his blood stream. It would kill him soon.

She pushed the bullet straight out, rather than letting it

travel back the way it had entered. She was more concerned about being quick, rather than causing the least amount of damage—any damage that she caused now he'd be able to heal from.

That is assuming he wasn't dead already. But that wasn't something she was willing to consider—the thought of having to tell the angry looking Vampire standing over her that she'd let his friend die made her shudder.

Giving herself a mental slap, she focused her concentration back on her patient.

The skin on the Vampires' stomach gave way with a small tear and the bullet popped out, falling to the dirty asphalt with a quiet *ping*.

She gave herself a few more minutes to try and repair some of the damage inside, making sure none of his vital organs had been nicked. It was exhausting work. She knew that it was time to stop when the ground beneath her started to tilt back and forth.

Stu growled to himself. The Witch looked like she was about to pass out next to her patient. What was taking so long? Was this normal? He'd never seen a healer work before.

She was short by human standards, barely even reaching his collarbone. Her light brown hair was pinned up in some type of clip that he'd seen females use before. She had stray strands of hair hanging in waves around her shoulders. Her silky blue dress pooled around her on the dirty pavement, slowly soaking up Arvid's blood. What was she doing wandering around such a dangerous part of town and dressed like that? Every hot-blooded male within a mile would've noticed her. It was a miracle that she hadn't caught the attention of a Soul Eater.

Even a human could've easily overpowered her.

She'd obviously been injured at some point; he could smell her blood. The urge to drink from her was riding him with a vengeance—which made no fucking sense because he'd fed just last week and shouldn't be exhibiting any signs of bloodlust. Most Vampires needed to have fresh blood every few weeks, but he could survive longer if need be.

Yet, all he could think about was sinking his fangs into the soft, sweet skin where her neck met her shoulder... And wasn't that fucked up, because a fellow soldier was fighting for his life at their feet.

Finally, she glanced up at Stu with a drained but triumphant look on her face.

"Done," she said, and reached out to pick up the bullet that had fallen from Arvid's chest. "He'll live. But you should give him blood. You know... Because he's a Vampire... That's what he needs..." Her words trailed off and some of the confidence started to fade from her expression. Could she read the hunger in his eyes? Was she scared of him? If she were smart, she would be.

Two large black SUVs turned into the alley, lighting up the figures standing around Arvid's unconscious body. Backup had arrived; Ros must have called them in.

The Witch stood up on legs that were clearly in danger of dumping her back on her ass. Stu reached out and grabbed her by the arm to pull her closer.

To prevent her from falling on Arvid, he told himself.

She winced, reminding him that he'd already grabbed her once and that she probably still had the bruises to show for it. Something akin to guilt soured his stomach, and his opinion of her went up when she straightened her spine and kept her discomfort to herself.

The doors on both SUVs opened, and four more soldiers got out. Vernar, the leader for the King's Army, approached Stu, while the three others bent down and lifted Arvid into one of the waiting vehicles. "Stu, what the hell happened?" he bit out, his eyes taking in the entire scene in a matter of seconds and stopping on the small Witch.

"Arvid took a bullet to the chest. Wouldn't have made it back to Bloddrikker in time to get it out. The civilian is a healer and took the bullet out while we waited for backup." He fisted his free hand in his coat pocket while Vernar gave her the once over. Then a twice over…

Stu silently swore every vulgarity he knew in his head, while the older Vampire continued to ogle the Witch. Or maybe he wasn't really staring at her… It was hard for Stu to see through the red haze that had started to cloud his vision.

"Hi, I'm Keltti." She looked like she was going to extend her hand to his leader but changed her mind at the last second.

"Bring her with us." Vernar walked away, knowing Stu would follow his instruction down to the last letter. Still holding her by the arm, Stu pulled her towards the closest SUV.

"Wait—what are you doing? Let go!" She tugged at his hand and dug her heels into the ground, but her protests didn't slow Stu's momentum in the least.

"Stop! You have no right to do this!" Her outrage was charming in its own way, and wasn't that a kick in the nuts. He refused to think too much about it. "Where are you taking me?"

He didn't bother to answer her questions; she'd find out soon enough.

CHAPTER 2

Keltti sat between two Vampires in the back of a dark SUV. Their large shoulders took up most of the space, leaving her little room to move.

It hadn't taken her long to realize they were all members of the King's Army. She didn't know much about the Vampires or their politics. As a child, she'd been told there were two types of Vampire: the blood drinking ones who established law and order among their kind, and the second type, known as Soul Eaters.

The majority of Vamps were typical, everyday folks who could be divided into lower, middle, and upper-class citizens. They were a lot like the humans they lived among, only with a much longer lifespan. And, their diet was a tad higher in iron.

The King's Army was in the same group, but in a class all of its own; these formidable Warriors were bred from a very select branch of the Vampire family tree. One didn't become a member of the King's Army; one was either *born* a member of the King's Army, or one wasn't. There was something in their genes that made them bigger and stronger than the average Vampire, and it could only be passed down from father to son.

The Vampire King, Erikki, ruled over all Vampire citizens, as well as policing the smaller minority groups of supernaturals, to ensure humans remained ignorant of their existence.

Vamps had plenty of food sources these days; humans

were plentiful in a big metropolis like Calgary, and for those who didn't care to dine out, there was a blood house. Keltti wasn't exactly sure how it worked; did they have delivery options too? It was none of her business, really.

Soul Eaters were another type of Vampire altogether. They were born as regular Vamps, but somewhere along the way they deviated from the straight and narrow and started draining the humans they fed from. Along with the gluttonous amount of blood they took, they also got the bonus of retaining a human's memories. The memories then drove them crazy, starting a vicious cycle of them trying to keep the voices of their victims from dominating their thoughts by gorging on more blood. They eventually descended into mindless animals, killing only to satisfy their endless appetite.

Both Warriors in the SUV were easily over a head taller than Keltti, and were dressed in long black coats that hid their amazingly strong, well-muscled bodies, as well as a fair share of concealed weapons. The Vampire to her right, Rostell, had introduced himself once the vehicle had started moving. "It was a good thing you were close by when Arvid went down. I thought I'd have to dig the bullet out myself." He shot her a smile before shyly looking away. His short spikey blond hair didn't look as if it had changed much since the eighties and he sported a black metal stud in one ear. His eyes were blue, and the moonlight reflecting off her dress made them appear to be the exact same aqua color. He glanced back down at her, and she fought the urge to smile back.

Is the big, bad Warrior shy? It was an oddly endearing thought.

Stu, the Vampire with the long black hair, kept his head turned towards the window, ignoring her completely. His expression was harsh, and his eyebrows furrowed as he continued to study his surroundings. The headlights from oncoming traffic occasionally washed away the shadows that clung to his strong jaw. His right hand rested close to his left hip, probably where he kept one of his guns. His thighs were the size of tree-trunks; she could feel the hard press of his tense muscles against her leg. The heat emanating from his body slid right through the thin fabric of her dress.

"Am I a prisoner?" she demanded of nobody in particular.

"No. Sarge just wants to ask you a few questions." Rostell's easy smile didn't hint at any deception, but Keltti reminded herself that she didn't know him. Just because someone said one thing doesn't mean they meant it.

If Norm, the pharmacist, had shown up to their date tonight like he said he would, she'd probably still be sipping wine by candlelight. Instead, she was wedged like a sardine between two huge male blocks of muscle, covered in Vampire blood, and scared out of her mind.

Stu had never been happier to see the underground parking garage at the castle. The Witch had fallen asleep almost immediately, her body relaxing into his from shoulder to thigh. The heat and scent coming from her were snaking their way around him in an intoxicating cloud that made it hard for him to think.

He pushed the door open and jumped out of the vehicle before it had even stopped moving. A fresh lungful of recirculated air helped clear his head. Once he felt as though he was back in control, he let himself turn back to the SUV. The Witch shuffled across the backseat and stumbled as she lowered herself to the ground.

"I'm fine." Her cold tone and the pointed look at his hand on her arm made him take a step back. And then he wondered when the fuck had he decided to help her out of the car in the first place?

He watched as her eyes, drowsy from her short nap, became alert and then return to their clear green. He'd thought they were darker in the alley. This was so fucked up—he was a god damn Warrior in the King's Army, not some pansy eye doctor.

Leaving her to follow or not, he marched towards the steel elevator doors and punched in a seven-digit code to access the lift. Behind him, he could hear Ros making small talk with the female. If the stupid elevator didn't come soon, he was going to end up punching the guy.

Stupid fucking bloodlust.

He'd hit the Blood Daughters' Manor in Kensington once his shift was over. The Keeper, Nakato, knew Stu's tastes, and was always accommodating. There were a variety of services available—not just the Blood Daughters who traditionally fed the King's Army. Blood was something Vamps depended on, but sex—that was just an awkward add on by the women that frequented the place. Not something he wanted to deal with. Just a condition of the blood exchange he negotiated with the coked-out housewives that Nakato brought in. They craved the thrill of taking a Warrior into their bed, while he needed the blood they could provide. At the end of the night, both parties parted ways satisfied.

He tugged at his chest holsters until they dug into the muscles of his back, then smacked at the damn elevator button again.

The Witch laughed at something Ros was saying, and the musical sound of her voice echoed across the parking garage. The cheerful *Bing!* as the elevator doors opened saved Stu from having to stick his daggers in his ears.

Keltti drummed her fingers idly on the metal table she sat at.

Not a prisoner, my butt!

She'd been escorted to a bare cement-block walled room, the thick steel door locking automatically behind her. Nothing but the table and two chairs for company. Dingy florescent lighting cast the room in a sickly yellow hue. And, she would bet her last dollar that the large rectangular mirror taking up one wall was a two-way. She wrestled with the urge to make faces at whoever was watching from the other side.

The door opened on well-oiled hinges and a tall brunette with a buzz cut walked in. He took the seat across from her, and Keltti recognized him as the Vampire from the alley that had ordered her to be taken here. His camo-print shirt and black cargo pants were neatly pressed. His boots were polished, without a single scuff or streak of dirt, despite his earlier visit to the filthy alley.

"I'm Captain Vernar. I want to thank you for your involvement tonight. Arvid is expected to make a full recovery."

Okay… this was so not what she was expecting to hear. She fought the urge to fidget and hoped that he'd get to the point soon; she was still tired from using her healing talents and wanted to go home.

"I'd like to offer you a unique opportunity with the King's Army on a subcontracted basis. I foresee great benefit to my soldiers by having you around to deal with the injuries that we experience on a nightly basis.

"Of course," he continued, "as a civilian, and not even a member of the Vampire population, all information would be provided on a need-to-know basis. You would be kept out of the direct line of fire and brought in once the battlefield is deemed safe. The benefits of working for us can be very lucrative."

Keltti let her mouth fall open before realizing that she had no idea what to say. She snapped it shut. Work for the King's Army? The *Vampire* King's Army?!? This was totally nuts—yet, here she was, actually considering what this could do for her future.

And why her? There were a number of covens in the country with far more skilled healers. Maybe the Vamps were unaware of the different skills that a Witch could be born with; healers being the most common. Keltti had a fair bit of power, but not much training. There were others who were stronger. Wiser. But Vampires and Witches didn't traditionally run in the same circles. She would have expected the King's Army to want the best—but then again, she was the only Witch that she knew of in such close proximity. Calgary tended to draw loners, and those who had nowhere else to go. Hiding among the humans was sometimes the only option for a supernatural in exile, regardless of whether it was self-imposed or not.

"I know this is somewhat unprecedented, forming an alliance between your people and mine, so I'd like for you to give it some thought before you give me an answer. Fighting the Rebels is a very worthy cause. I'll have one of my patrols give you a ride home on their way out."

And just like that he had dismissed her. He left without a backwards glance and she was left speechless staring at the empty chair he had just vacated. Jeez, this guy must be used to getting his way. It hadn't even occurred to him that she might have a few questions for him to answer.

Rostell entered before she could even think to check if the door had been left unlocked. "Hey. Sarge said to take you home. Ready to go?"

Stu sat in the back seat of the idling SUV, impatiently drumming his fingers on his leg. Tor and Ros were headed out to patrol the residential communities that Soul Eaters occasionally stalked, and Stu was catching a ride to the Blood Daughters' Manor.

His dry parched throat made talking difficult, but Tor wasn't much of a talker, so he kept his mouth shut and his dark thoughts to himself. Being around the damn sexy Witch tonight had only brought on the inevitable. The strain of almost losing someone he served with was also adding to the situation. Probably.

Shit—just when he thought the night couldn't get any worse, he caught sight of Ros striding across the lot with the Witch in tow. His fangs bit into his bottom lip and he tasted blood. And son of a bitch, didn't that just make him even thirstier.

The blonde Warrior opened the back door and motioned for her to climb in before he claimed the front seat for himself. The familiar smell of springtime and honey settled over Stu's senses as she did up her seatbelt, and he fought against the urge to put a few more inches between them—partly because he didn't want the other males to pick up on how distracted he was, but mostly because he didn't want to admit that particular weakness to himself. And it was definitely a weakness. There was a pile of fucking paperwork waiting for him upstairs, and he needed to debrief Arvid and Ros so he could fill Sarge in on their monumental clusterfuck of a night. But first things first— he needed to get to the Blood Daughters' Manor.

Tor turned around in the driver's seat and glanced at the Witch in question.

"This is Torjben. Tor, this is Keltti. We're givin' her a ride home." Stu was snapped out of his internal musings by Ros's introduction to the Warrior behind the wheel, and the Witch's murmured acknowledgement. He could feel her exhaustion from where he was sitting, and he wondered if she'd fall asleep next to him again. Why the fuck did he even care?

Tor took his damn sweet time putting the vehicle in gear and guiding it out of the underground lot. The location of Bloddrikker Castle was common knowledge among most of the supernatural community; there was no need to hide it from her. He tried to concentrate on the pockets of forested hills as they gave way to the sprawling reaches of the big city. Signs of human development were everywhere. And where there were humans, there would be Soul Eaters.

All Vampires, including the Soul Eaters, would burn in direct sunlight. Soon, they would be confined to whatever primitive means of shelter they could find: abandoned buildings, underground tunnels, the sewer, or caves. Once their minds had become too fractured from the onslaught of memories from their victims, any semblance of a normal life fell apart. They stopped going to work and lost their source of income. The homes they'd worked hard for would get abandoned, and they'd essentially become homeless.

Blood was always a necessary part of life, but once a Vampire let bloodlust take over, it was a short trip downhill, to draining their next victim and consuming their soul. That was a choice you couldn't come back from. There was no rehabilitating a Soul Eater.

Stu broke out in a sweat just thinking about it. There's no way he should have waited this long to drink. It was a dangerous game, taking blood with so much frustration pumping through his body right now. It would be too easy to lose control and take it all tonight. Become one of the very monsters he pledged his King to purge the world of.

No fucking way he should be around anyone right now. He was irritable as hell; his fellow soldiers had picked up on his foul mood earlier and had been giving him a wide berth.

A blinding light filled the body of the SUV; half a second later another vehicle smashed into the driver side while the curtain airbags all simultaneously deployed with a *bang*.

Someone in the front seat let out an expletive that was cut off by the tearing of metal as they ripped through the guard rail and tore down the steep embankment into a strand of trees. They stopped with a sudden *crunch* against a wide elm tree; the only thing moving in the sudden quiet was the airbag powder slowly falling through the air.

Stu shoved the shock aside and flew into motion. "Status!" he barked at his soldiers.

"Tor's down." Ros reported as he pulled his gun and jumped from the front seat.

Stu followed, after a few good hits with his shoulder to the crumpled door. He dragged the Witch behind him as he went. Ros met them around the front of the vehicle, dragging Tor over his shoulder like a two-hundred-and-fifty-pound side of beef.

Bullets ripped up the ground around them as someone on the road above opened fire. The damn Sterken were becoming more than just a pain in his ass; two gutsy confrontations in one night was unheard of.

"Down!" Stu shouted, pushing the Witch into the trees next to them. A quick glance around the tree trunk revealed that they were outnumbered. Ros must have reached the same conclusion; his voice came over the comm link asking for backup. Stu returned a round of fire, trying to keep them from advancing on his position.

"Go! Into the trees!" he yelled, gesturing them further away from the road. Ros waited for Stu's signal, then took off with Tor, running for the next available cover. The Witch watched hesitantly, clearly afraid. *"Go!"* Stu told her, putting his body further into the line of fire to provide her with a small amount of coverage. *"Move it!"*

She took off sprinting towards where Ros waited, and he held his position until he knew she was out of range of their bullets. He could hear the Rebels scrambling down the steep embankment; it wouldn't be long until they breached his small refuge among the trees.

Behind him, Ros's gun rang out, slowing the enemy's advancement. "Come on!" the Witches voice cried, and he turned to see her shooting towards the Rebel's as they tried to corral him. "Stu!" The frantic tone in her voice snapped him out of his thoughts and he didn't hesitate a second longer, taking off with his thighs pumping. The grass around his feet exploded with bullets as he dove behind the boulder to where she waited.

Ros had Tor slung over his shoulder, ready to take off. "We gotta go, there's too many of them."

Stu considered standing their ground, knowing a fight would help take the edge off his needs. But Tor was injured, and there was the Witch to consider; he appreciated her picking up arms to help but it was clear she didn't know what she was doing. No, they wouldn't stand much of a chance without backup. He nodded and signaled for Ros to head further into the trees.

Keltti tried to keep her shaking hands steady as she

squeezed another shot off. There probably weren't many bullets left in her borrowed gun, but Stu had already taken down five of the Rebels.

Just one left, she thought to herself. At least, she was pretty sure it was just one. It was hard to tell with the trees blocking out the moonlight.

They had fallen into a predictable pattern of movement: Rostell and Keltti would head deeper into the forest, while Stu covered them. Then Keltti would return fire at the Rebels to cover Stu's quick dash to catch up with them.

She motioned over her shoulder that Rostell should go on without her. Lying on her belly under a thick canopy of leaves, she would be nearly invisible to the human eye. Hopefully, to Vampire eyes, too. She lay motionless, waiting for Stu to turn and run in her direction. Clearly the Rebel was waiting too, because, when Stu took off running, he stepped out from behind a thick tree trunk to take a shot.

She could do this… It was just like shooting gophers as a child. The little buggers would eat up all the grass that the sheep relied on for grazing. She had been helping protect her flock then, and she would do the same now. Nothing to see here folks; just a shepherd looking out for her flock. Of Vampires. With a handgun. A really *big* handgun. Filled with poisoned bullets.

Keltti let out the breath that she'd been holding, and pulled the trigger. Time slowed to a crawl as the bullet whizzed past Stu. She saw the expression on his face change; he was probably thinking she was shooting at him. She felt mildly guilty, until the bullet ended its journey lodged in the Rebel's leg. He lost his balance and fell forward, and before he could get up, Stu turned and unleashed two more bullets into his chest.

Grinning, Keltti disentangled herself from the bush she'd been hiding under and approached Stu where he stood with both arms outstretched, pointing his guns in two different directions, searching for nearby threats. But, he wouldn't find any—because she had helped take down the last one!

She wanted to pump her fists in the air and let the whole world know she'd played a part in tonight's battle. She wanted to throw back her head and scream of her victory until the entire forest heard.

Instead, she politely handed over her borrowed gun and kept her mouth shut. Tonight had been an amazing, epic, adrenaline-filled adventure for her, but it was probably just an average Friday night for the male standing in front of her. Squealing like a high-school cheerleader would probably be frowned upon by the stoic Warriors—and something she could do when she was alone.

Her instincts as a healer demanded that she comfort and aid those in need of help, but this was so unlike anything she had ever imagined. This was putting her own safety directly between her flock and whatever threatened it. Her *Vampire* flock. Oh Goddess, the Vamps would probably shoot her if they knew what she was thinking.

The Vampire looked down at her. His eyes glinted harshly in the moonlight, a warning that he was even more dangerous than the Vampire's that had attacked them. And didn't that just make her want to…

Yeah, she wanted to kiss him. Not a friendly kiss, but a passionate one, full of the life that she was grateful for. Would he meet her halfway? Judging by his feral expression, he was more interested in killing something with his bare hands than humoring a lonely Witch.

What the heck was she thinking, anyway? This was so unlike her.

Every inch of that rock-hard body… And… Did I really just shoot *someone?*

There was probably a clinical term for what was happening to her right now, something to do with adrenaline, post traumatic stress, and just being so damn grateful to be alive. Making rational decisions following a significant trauma was difficult—but none of the terms or jargon her brain was throwing out mattered.

She bit down on her lip to keep a hysterical giggle from escaping, and took a step back.

Yeah, he'd definitely shoot her if he knew what she was thinking.

CHAPTER 3

Stu groaned and tried to reign his emotions back in. His hunger was making him dizzy.

Yeah, the hunger. That's it. Fucking hunger is all.

The little Witch smiled up at him, her gaze demure and innocent; she clearly had no idea how enticing he found her presence. His fangs ached, and he swallowed thickly. This damn night couldn't end soon enough.

"Stu…. *Stu!* Dude, snap out of it!" He reluctantly pulled his gaze from the sexy Witch, ready to tear the head off of whoever had dared to interrupt him. His face must've conveyed his displeasure, because Ros raised his hands in the air and took a step back. "Dude, backups almost here… Yeah, I'll just check on Tor." He turned away before Stu could comment.

He scanned the woods for threats, keeping his gaze anywhere—everywhere—but on her. What was his Goddamn problem? He needed fucking blood. Yeah, a few pints of O-neg and he'd be good to go.

The glow of high-powered flashlights shone through the trees in the direction from which they had come. The arrival of backup helped to clear his head, and he took a step back from the Witch.

"Oh, my goodness, you're bleeding!" She exclaimed, grabbing his hand that was sticky with blood. Her gaze climbed to his left shoulder and she must have caught sight of the hole that had been ripped in his coat. He shrugged and brushed off her attempts to get a look under the fabric.

"It went straight through, it's fine."

"You were *shot*?!? And you didn't say anything?" Stu started to shrug again, but thought better of causing any more damage to the injury.

"It wasn't bothering me."

And I had other things on my mind…

"Stu! Sit down, you're going into shock. Let me look." He had to smile while she tried to manhandle him into sitting on a broken log.

"It's fine—" he started, but was quickly cut off by Keltti's angry look.

"It's *not* fine. Captain Vernar offered me a position as your official healer while you're out in the field, and I have decided to accept." She stood a little taller and put her hands on her hips. "So, stop acting like an infant; I am ordering you to sit down and shut up while I take a look at your shoulder."

She lifted her chin, daring him to argue. Damn she was beautiful. And bluffing. There's no way in hell the Captain would do something so careless without discussing it with him first. As Vernar's second in command, Stu had a hand in all major decisions.

"It's true. That's why Sarge had her brought back to Bloddrikker," Ros said as he returned. He sounded apologetic, but the twinkle in his eyes told Stu he was definitely enjoying himself.

Ranvald and Kyenel silently stepped through the trees. The Witch jumped, almost falling over in her surprise at their sudden arrival, but Stu caught her. Her Witch's senses were akin to that of a human, and she wouldn't have known that they were close until they appeared out of the darkness only a few feet away.

Kye walked over to the body of the Rebel and flipped it over with the toe of his boot. He raised an eyebrow questioningly. "We found five more between here and the road, plus this pile of scum." Stu confirmed his headcount with a nod.

"There must have been another one driving; their vehicle was gone from the road," Kye added.

The Witch looked back and forth between them before she marched over to where Tor lay. She ignored Ros as he stood over them with his guns drawn, scanning the surrounding forest for further threats. She silently laid her hands on the injured soldier.

Stu growled, and Kye and Ran both raised their guns higher, ready for whatever threat Stu had perceived. But the only current threat to any of the Warriors was the possibility of Stu's boot connecting with Tor's head. Because seeing the Witch's hands all over another male was just wrong. So fucking *wrong*.

He refused to look too closely at the fact that Tor was unconscious.

Or the fact that she was the closest source of blood that he was so anxious for.

So, he sat on the rotting log while the Witch murmured to herself. He tried to focus on the throb of his shoulder, instead of all the inappropriate ideas his grey-matter was throwing out. His response to the shy little Witch was baffling. Realistically he knew she was too classy, too elegant, to be with a male that literally waded through blood and bodies on a daily basis. He needed to get his shit together.

He growled again and the other three Warriors gave him looks ranging from confusion to amusement.

"Ahh… just fuck off." He told them, not wanting to explain what was wrong with him.

So, so many fucking things that were wrong.

Hopefully, they'd chalk it up to bloodlust and leave him alone.

Tor quietly moaned and started to move. The Witch looked up at them and smiled. "He's okay. Just a concussion, and no internal damage." The small, tired lines around her eyes betrayed her weariness from the small healing she had just done.

"We should get out of here; the sun will be up soon." Ranvald stated what most of them had already been thinking. The woods were already starting to get lighter.

They took off back the way that they had come. Stu expected the Witch to fuss over his bullet wound, but she didn't say a word. Instead, she seemed to be avoiding him, sticking close to Tor as if he were about to faint. Jeez. The guy had a concussion, not some terminal illness that would cause him to drop dead at any moment.

For the hundredth time that night, Stu wondered what the hell was wrong with him.

Keltti traipsed through the woods in her ripped, blood-stained dress. She could only imagine how bad she looked.

The broken mangled shape of the wrecked vehicle came into view, and she breathed a sigh of relief. Another dark SUV waited for them on the road above. Any further, and she would have fallen asleep on her feet.

She watched Stu slide into the front passenger seat, and she shook her head. "Nope, you're riding in the back where I can take a look at your shoulder. Let's go." He glowered at her and clenched his jaw as if holding back words, but he kept his mouth shut and climbed into the back of the vehicle.

She followed him into the cramped space, trying not to let her face reveal her surprise that he had actually listened to her demands. It was surreal having the power to exert her wishes over another's. Especially when it was a big, dominant male who was used to getting his way. Using her healing to help the Vampire King's Army was turning out to have perks.

There wasn't much room in the third row; Stu's massive body took up what little space there was. Keltti wedged herself in, trying to remain professional while pressed up against him. She laid her hands on his chest and bicep, pretending not to notice when he flinched.

She let her powers take over, delving through the thick

layers to get to the Warrior's injury. It was an angry pulsing streak that followed the path of the bullet straight through from front to back. No toxic poisons from the bullet to breakdown, just damage to the tissue and muscles. Her body focused on his, mending as much of the damage as she could before they reached the castle.

Judging by how close they were to dawn, there wouldn't be time to take her home, and she'd have to spend the day at Bloddrikker. Not really something that she wanted to do, especially when there was a hot bath and clean clothes waiting for her at home. Of course, she'd need to sleep soon. Probably for most of the day. And if she couldn't sleep, she'd see if she could get a cab. She was a practical city girl, after all.

Would they make her stay in that awful cell again? She sure hoped not.

The armoured SUV arrived in the underground garage with just minutes to spare before the sun crested the horizon. Nothing like riding the thin line between life and third-degree burns.

The Vampires climbed out of the vehicles, still discussing the night's attack. It was a bold, brazen move by the Rebels; far more organized and offensive than anything they had encountered before. Stu could feel weariness setting into his bones. Some days it didn't feel like they were making any progress at all. They'd taken out six of the enemy, but at what cost? If Tor had hit his head any harder, he'd have ended up as a vegetable for life. And, there was the Witch to think about… she wasn't a part of their conflict, not really. But they'd put her in harms way regardless. That was fucking unacceptable.

Stu and the Witch left everyone else on the first basement level and rode the elevator to the top floor where the onsite suites were located. She leaned wearily against the cool metal wall and her eyes fluttered shut as the elevator hummed upward.

"Witch." Stu reached out and touched the soft skin on her bicep, eliciting a startled gasp. "You're going to fall asleep on your feet," he said, more harshly than he intended to.

"Sorry, just tired." She yawned, displaying her slight curves as she stretched upwards, reminding him that, until the sun went down, they'd both be trapped in the castle for the day. Technically, he could take blood from anyone, but he preferred to feed from females. And right now, he was hurting for a taste of the delectable Witch next to him.

"And it's Keltti…. My name—it's Keltti." He let her name roll through his mind a few times, deciding that it fit her nicely. Short and sweet, it would roll off his tongue slowly, like expensive scotch.

The elevator deposited them on the third floor and Stu didn't wait for her permission. He scooped her up into his arms and strode down the hall towards the guest rooms. The Warrior's rooms were in the opposite direction, not that it mattered—he knew his limits and wasn't about to torture himself by having her any closer than necessary.

"What are you doing!?" Keltti exclaimed, sounding like a scandalized librarian. Stu hid the small smile that would have exposed his satisfaction at shocking her.

"You're tired and are going to fall on your stubborn little ass." Her weak protests fell on deaf ears, and he felt the exact moment when her entire body relaxed and gave in to him. After shouldering his way past the thick wooden door, he set her on the recliner in the main sitting room.

"I need to sleep," she whispered softly, clearly overwhelmed by whatever she saw on his face. He knew he was staring, but he couldn't seem to tear his eyes away. Vaguely some part of him wondered what was going through the little Witch's head. She'd want to run screaming if she knew what was in his.

"Can I shower first?... The dried blood…" Her sentence trailed off as if she was reading his thoughts. He stood perfectly still, not wanting to scare her any further. Hell, was

28

she actually *asking for permission* to get naked? He swallowed heavily, and nodded towards the door to the bathroom, not trusting himself to use words—not that he could get any past the elongated fangs filling his mouth.

His eyes followed her across the room until the door closed between them with a *click!* Holy Hell, he needed to distract himself before he decided to march himself in there and join her. Naked. Together.

Yeah, that couldn't happen… he had more control than that. He hoped.

Keltti finished washing her bra and panties in the sink and hung them on the towel rack to dry. They should be good to go by evening. She peeled the ripped and bloodied dress over her head and tossed it in the corner, never wanting to see the stupid thing again.

She wasn't sure what to expect in an ancient castle, but the bathroom was clean and modern. The water came out steaming hot with just the right pressure. Every exhausted muscle in her body sighed with pleasure and relaxed into the simple joy of becoming clean. The soap was subtle and spicy, reminding her of the heady scent of male Vampire.

She shook her head, wondering what had gotten into her earlier. Wanting to kiss a stranger was so unlike her. But then she'd seen the way he had looked at her before she took her leave to shower. Anger and frustration and maybe a bit of confusion? She didn't know what it meant, but he clearly wasn't putting off any warm fuzzy vibes towards her. Maybe he was resentful at being her glorified babysitter for the day? Well, it was lucky for him that she didn't need one.

And she certainly wasn't going to throw herself at him.

It had been ten years since she'd been with anyone, and she was more than ready to try again—but she was also prepared to be patient. She could wait until she met the right man. Online dating had seemed like the best option—that's how she'd found Norm. Her expectations tonight hadn't been ridiculously high; have a nice meal, get to know each other in person instead of the back and forth messaging they'd done up until that point, and possibly a good night kiss. If she was totally honest with herself, any personal connection would've been acceptable. The lonely, empty feelings she usually carried around had recently gotten stronger and harder to bear.

But if she wasn't careful, she'd get a repeat of what had happened with her last boyfriend (if one could even call him that). Trent had been a software sales rep for the larger medical companies in Western Canada. They'd met at a soup and sandwich shop downtown during the lunch rush. The place had been full, and he had asked to share her table. He'd been charming and flirty without ever crossing the line into inappropriate. She'd had no experience with the opposite sex and had lapped up the attention.

Their brief courtship had lasted two weeks and ended once he'd gotten what he wanted from her. After, he had laughed at her naivety and left.

"Thanks for tonight but you know, you're not really the sticking-around-for type."

She'd had nothing to show for it but a handful of pretty words and empty promises.

No—that wasn't true. She had gotten something much more important out of the experience. Learning the hard way was sometimes the best way to get the message through; she hadn't forgotten that particular lesson and never would.

She'd have to be careful around Stu. A male like that was dangerous for a girl like her, who still wasn't sure how to keep her heart out of the equation.

Stu paced back and forth in the small sitting room of his sparsely furnished suite.

He'd left a clean shirt and workout pants sitting on the bed in the guest room. He'd shamefully stood and listened to the sound of the shower running for longer than he'd like to admit, then hightailed it out of there. His thirst and desire for her were all tangled up in his head, making him uncertain and cranky as hell.

This is bullshit, he told himself for the dozenth time. He was a century old Vampire for God's sake. He needed to figure out what the hell was wrong with him. The little Witch was right down the hall for fuck sake, and he was out here pacing like a juvenile with his dick in his hand.

Figuratively of course. Because there's no way in hell he'd ever want to be caught in that position.

He needed to find something productive to do, instead of torturing himself like this. He'd never been hit so hard by the bloodlust before. It was fucking unacceptable. Downright pathetic.

He knew there was a mountain of paperwork downstairs waiting for his attention, not to mention the fun conversation he needed to have with Sarge regarding the fact that he'd hired a healer without consulting him. A fucking *civilian*, completely untrained in the art of combat or field situations. Although, he grudgingly had to admit that she'd handled herself well tonight in two separate field situations. Still, as the Captain's second in command, Stu would have insisted that Kye run a thorough background check to ferret out any possible connections between her and the Vampire populace. Even the slightest contact between her and someone thought to be sympathetic to the Sterken, no matter how innocent or coincidental, would have been a red flag. It wasn't unheard of for other supernatural races to chafe under the restrictions that were imposed by the Vampire King and enforced by the Warriors in the King's Army.

He put his hand on the doorknob and before he could remind himself of the hundred reasons not to, he opened the door and stalked down the hall. The low-slung sweats that he'd thrown on were a courtesy for any of the other males he might run into.

Stopping in front of the guest room, he pushed with his Vampire senses, hoping to hear any sound that would indicate that she was still awake. But there were no soft footfalls or even the restless crinkle of sheets from someone tossing side to side in bed. She must be asleep, all warm and lush under the covers, her breathing calm and even. He stood, torn between leaving and staying to see if she'd be receptive to his attentions.

He tried to remind himself that she wasn't just some desperate rich wife looking to forget about her mundane existence and ignorant husband by climbing on top of him. She was a Witch. A *healer* for God's sake. Healers were full of goodness and compassion, nothing like the females he was used to.

And while most Witch's were wild and promiscuous, this one didn't seem to fit the mold. She was young and modest and probably a little naïve. Even if she did agree to settle for a male like him, she probably wouldn't understand what she was signing on for. Males in the King's Army weren't just trained for the position, they were bred for it. Centuries of selective breeding had produced the strongest, most virile males possible to serve as Warriors for the species. Along with their heightened senses, increased speed and powerful strength, came a hearty appetite for carnal pleasures. It probably had something to do with continuing the bloodlines—any male lucky enough to find his life mate would already be well experienced and able to produce an heir, thus adding to the dwindling Vampire race.

No, someone as soft and delicate as her was made for better things than one night with a male who spent his nights roaming the killing field with blood on his boots.

He fisted his hand before letting it fall away from the doorknob.

CHAPTER 4

After five hours of tossing and turning, Keltti conceded defeat and crawled out of bed groggy and a little grumpy. While sleep was the best way to replenish her body after using a large amount of magic in such a short amount of time, food would work too.

Still wearing the borrowed shirt and pants she'd slept in, she located the elevator and rode it down to the first floor, where she hoped the kitchen would be. Aside from the fact that there was no tacky music playing, it looked like a normal elevator.

Stepping into a dimly-lit hallway, Keltti stopped and tried to get her bearings. There was no helpful map marked with a YOU ARE HERE next to a little red star. The decor was an exact opposite to the floor she'd just come from. Instead of wood panelling and elegant wallpaper, there was a definite upscale office vibe with all the frosted glass and gleaming metal. The floor was polished concrete and felt cold beneath her bare feet.

Keltti chose to go right, following a dull rhythmic sound until the hallway ended at a large set of double doors that were ajar. Inside, she could see a large open space that looked like an elementary school gymnasium. Blue vinyl mats covered half the hardwood, while the other half was filled with an assortment of weights and cardio machines. Two male Vampires threw punches at each other in the center of the mats, while another one watched from the sidelines. She instantly recognized Stu, even though his back was to her. His long hair and aggressive posture were unmistakable as he dodged a kick aimed at his head, then swept his foot behind his opponent's knee to knock him over.

"Are you lost?" Keltti jumped at the voice that came from directly behind her, and spun around to find a male standing next to her.

Embarrassed at being caught spying, she had to clear her throat a few times before she managed to choke out, "Sorry, I was just looking for the kitchen."

The Vampire smiled, and she recognized him as the Warrior who had carried Tor through the woods after the accident. Rostell, if was remembering right. "You should be resting," she told him, cringing when she realized how bossy she sounded.

"Nah, I'm good to go. Vampire healing, and all that." His smile brightened a little, so she must not have offended him. "I threw some snacks in the oven, they'll be ready in a few minutes if you're hungry?"

She nodded her thanks. "That sounds great."

The sounds of flesh hitting flesh continued to pour from the open doors, and Keltti glanced back to where the males were pummelling each other with single minded focus.

"You were impressive tonight." The soft words brought her attention back to the male standing next to her. "Most civilians wouldn't have been able to keep their cool like you did."

"Thanks." She looked away first, uncomfortable with the admiration in his eyes.

"Where did you learn to shoot?"

"There were a lot of gophers where I grew up; I knew how to use a .22 by the time I was nine." He chuckled and she felt herself starting to relax in the presence of the huge Warrior. "Yours was a little harder to figure out."

"Yeah, the kickback can be a real bear. How are your wrists?"

"They're fine," she lied. They were still sore from firing

the giant gun, but she didn't want to complain about something so trivial. "So, what was in the bullet that shot Arvid? It was poisoning him but I didn't think Vampire's could be poisoned."

"We don't actually know what the Rebels use in their bullets, but they sure hurt like a son of a b—ah, gun. We use mercury and polonium, so it's probably something similarly toxic." He must have sensed that his casual talk of getting shot with lethal amounts of poison was upsetting her, because he hurried to reassure her with, "They pack a real punch at close range and usually just go right through. It's just the ones that get stuck inside us that can be deadly." Which wasn't actually reassuring at all.

"How many of you live here?" Keltti tried to force her mind away from thoughts of more Warrior's getting shot and relying on her for help. She was just a novice Witch, how much help could she really be?

"There are seven of us at Bloddrikker. The King established it as an outpost in the 1870s to deal with the rising number of Vampires immigrating to the new world."

Keltti blinked at that little tidbit of Vampire trivia. "Just seven?"

"Yeah. There used to be more; we've lost some good males since the Rebellion sprung up." He ran a hand across the tall blonde spikes of his hair, probably unaware that she could hear the layer of grief in his voice.

"But you killed six of them tonight." Plus the one that Stu had shot in the alley, but it seemed tacky to mention.

He shrugged. "Six Rebels is hardly a drop in the bucket. There are probably still a hundred more, just in Calgary alone. And they're always recruiting, so their numbers keep growing."

"What? That's crazy! How does your King expect you to take on a hundred Vampires?" Her ire rose at the thought of what these males must face on a nightly basis.

Rostell slanted her a wolfish grin that made her heartrate increase. "We're the King's Warriors." Something about the way he said it, with such confidence and pride, convinced her that the Rebels didn't stand a chance against these terrifying Warriors.

Whap! Whap! Whap! Stu's fists collided with the heavy bag, the sound punctuated by his breath, sawing its way in and out of his lungs. Jab, jab, upper cut, jab. Don't think about it. Hook, hook, upper cut, jab. Keep your mind on the bag. Jab, feint left, jab, jab. Don't fucking think about her!

After running from the guest suites like a fucking toddler, he'd sought refuge in the training room downstairs.

His arms felt like overcooked pasta, and his knuckles burned where sweat ran into the open cuts from working the heavy bag. His long hair, held together with an elastic band, stuck to the skin between his shoulder blades. Two encounters with the Rebels in one night, combined with the impromptu sparring session with Kye, should have knocked him on his ass. But there he was, hammering away like the bag had personally wronged him.

His sudden bloodlust made no sense. He could call Nakato to have a donor sent over to the castle; it wouldn't raise any eyebrows—the Warrior's did it regularly when they were injured and couldn't wait until sunset to visit the Blood Daughters' Manor. After a split second of indecision, he almost discarded the idea on an angry exhale. Just the thought of drinking from a random human filled his mouth with the taste of ash. But he was Warrior first and foremost, and knew if he didn't get blood soon, he'd be useless out in the field. And judging by the way the Rebels were ramping up their attacks, he was going to need all the strength he could muster; any weakness on his part would make him a liability to his brothers.

With a bleeding hand, he pulled out his cell and made the call to Nakato.

It would be an hour before the donor arrived, so he hit the showers and let the hot water sluice over his body, clearing any of Keltti's lingering scent from his body.

With a start, he realized there was one explanation for his sudden bloodlust. One simple reason that would also explain the aggression and possession he felt when he was around the Witch—she had the potential to be his true mate.

It was rare; so rare, that he hadn't even considered the possibility until now.

But, no—no, it wasn't possible.

Was it?

Any male would be honored to find himself a life mate; most spent centuries hopefully awaiting theirs. Stu had given up long ago. He'd found his calling by dedicating his life to the King's Army; waiting for his own personal slice of heaven to arrive on a silver platter had seemed self-centred and improbable. Instead, he had chosen a different type of selfish: extracting revenge on the Sterken bastards that had murdered his mother.

With his head hanging under the hot spray, he thought through his limited knowledge of Vampire mating.

He'd been raised by his mother and father, who had been mated for well over two centuries. They had immigrated here from their homeland of Norway, under the command of King Erikki, to establish a Vampire stronghold in the new world. Seven years into the construction of Bloddrikker Castle, Stu had been born. He was the first; and his birth had been cause for weeks of celebration.

The mating mark was exclusive to Vamps, and it could only appear when a couple bonded with blood and sex— but the most important thing, his father had once explained, was the right combination of pheromones, chemistry, and biology. His mother had called it "love," and the two males had snorted at her romantic tendencies. Still, Stu didn't miss the heated way his father had followed her with his eyes as she'd left the room.

His father's mating mark had been a bold cluster of blade-shaped crescents, and sat high on the left side of his arse. Stu had seen it many times, never truly grasping the importance of it until he was well into his fifties. And any time he'd brought up his mothers, she'd blushed and told him primly that it was for his father's eyes only. Enough said—he wasn't letting his mind wander down that particular road. Only Vampires had the gift of giving a mating mark; other supernaturals had their own mating rites.

Stu groaned and tried to force the dizzying thoughts from his head. He needed to focus on more important things—like figuring out what the hell the Rebels were planning. Two blatant attacks in one night were unheard of; the bastards had something in the works and Stu needed to get ahead of whatever they were planning before it gathered momentum.

Whatever this thing with the Witch was, however improbable, he'd deal with it later.

Pizza was the greatest equalizer ever invented. It had the ability to bring people from all walks of life together; in this particular instance, one hesitant Witch and a group of very large, very intimidating male Vampires.

After Keltti had followed Ros into the kitchen and helped him remove six large pizzas from the wall ovens, two other Warriors, Kyenel and Ranvald, had followed the delicious aroma.

"And then she shoves Stu out of the way." Across the large kitchen island, Ros made a dramatic pushing motion that made his biceps flex to obscene proportions as he told the other males about Keltti's arrival in the alley.

"I didn't *shove* him—" Keltti tried to interject.

"Then she puts her hands on Arvid and the whole stinking alley starts to smell like grass and trees." Ros cut her a hesitant smile as he finished his story before helping himself to another steaming piece of pizza.

"Why did it smell like grass and trees?" Kye asked.

Ros thought for a minute before guessing, "Witch magic?"

In a move that was eerily synchronized, the Warriors all turned to Keltti with questioning looks on their faces. She froze with her pizza halfway to her mouth, feeling like a deer caught in the headlights of three really big trucks. "Healing magic?" she suggested with a shrug. She'd never realized that her healing had a scent.

"Then what?" Ranvald asked as he scooped up another huge slice.

"Then the bullet popped out. Stu looked like he was going to lose his sh—ah, blow a gasket; I didn't know if he was going to strangle her or kiss her."

"Definitely strangle her—have you ever known Stu to pass up the chance to start a fight?" Another male walked in, earning a few high-fives and claps on his shoulder as he worked his way closer to where Keltti was standing. It took her a few seconds to recognize the short dark curls and chiselled jaw as belonging to the Vampire she'd saved the night before. He didn't stop until he was right in front of Keltti, and she hesitantly returned the smile he was giving her.

"Thank you." He spoke softly, with an ocean of sincerity in his vivid blue eyes.

"You're welcome." She wanted to take a step back, to put some space between the huge male and herself, but her back was already pressed into the marble countertop. Suddenly aware of the hush that had fallen over the room, Keltti stammered, "Ah—I'm Keltti."

"Arvid." He flashed her a rakish grin, full of straight white teeth that belonged in a toothpaste ad.

Uncomfortable with the intensity of his gaze, she slid her eyes over his loose t-shirt and sweat pants, looking for signs that he'd been shot. "How's your injury?"

"Good as new," he told her as he gripped the bottom of his shirt and tugged it over his head.

She felt a flash of embarrassment at the sudden appearance of his ripped chest, but it was quickly replaced with curiosity when she caught sight of the jagged scars.

Both holes had completely healed, leaving only small pink marks where the bullet had entered and exited.

"Wow." She'd never seen so much damage healed so fast before.

"Yeah, I get that a lot from the ladies." He smirked.

Keltti snorted and rolled her eyes. "That's not what I meant—I'm just surprised how fast you healed."

"Sure," Arvid winked and tugged his shirt back on before reaching for a slice of pizza.

Grateful to have some personal space again, Keltti relaxed against the counter and let the sound of friendly banter wash over her. The Warriors were obviously a close-knit group and reminded her of her former coven. It was the same sense of family, the same feeling of belonging—just with a lot more profanity and testosterone.

The conversation turned back to "those Rebel bastards," and Keltti shook off her inner musings. If she was going to be working for them, she needed to understand what they were up against.

"They've got to have eyes on us; that shit they pulled tonight was planned," Kye mused.

"How? Are they accessing the GPS in the vehicles?" Arvid contemplated with his mouth full of pizza.

Kye made a disgusted scoffing sound. "Not possible. I installed my own software in the SUVs and everyone's cell; I'm the only one that can track them now." He narrowed his eyes thoughtfully, then looked over to where Keltti was standing. "Unless... Where's your cell?"

Keltti stupidly patted the front of her pants until she realized the borrowed clothes didn't have pockets. "I don't know. I lost it—maybe in the alley or running through the woods?"

"You think they tracked her phone?" Ros asked.

"Probably not, nobody knew she was here." Kye crossed his arms and tilted his head as he continued to study her. "Unless they saw a vehicle leave the castle and *then* picked up the signal from her cell, they would have known what road you were on and radioed ahead to the group that ambushed you."

"That's a lot of ifs." Ranvald commented.

"There's no way Harbin is capable of orchestrating something that complex." Ros interjected.

"Who's Harbin?" Keltti asked in confusion.

"The self-proclaimed leader of the Rebel's movement." Kye spit the words out like the name itself tasted bad in his mouth.

"He's one manipulative son of a—ah, gun." Ros added. "A real pain in our butts."

"But nowhere near smart enough to pull off an ambush like what we saw tonight." Ranvald added.

"But, why?" Keltti asked. "What does he stand to gain from hurting any of you?"

Kye shrugged. "New world order. Without anyone to uphold the laws the King established, Vampires would be free to do whatever they wanted and put whoever they want into power. Most likely, Harbin is just running the branch here in North America and their true leader is pulling his strings from back in Norway."

"Of course, knowing Harbin, there's a good chance he's just looking to create chaos so he can run around unchecked." Arvid added. "Most of his followers are sick of hiding in the shadows and want the world to know that Vampires exist."

"That's crazy!" Keltti exclaimed. "If the humans find out about Vampires—"

"Then they'll find out about Witches, and every other supernatural that just wants to scrape out a living? Yeah, that's exactly why we're trying to stop this stupid movement before it gets out of control." The determination in Kye's silver gaze was nearly tangible and Keltti took an involuntary step backwards.

"And there's only seven of you?" She asked in exasperation. How in the world did the Vampire King expect seven males to stop an entire Rebellion? Her ire for their leader continued to rise as she thought about how Arvid had nearly died. And how Tor and Stu had been practically indifferent to their injuries, like it was no big deal to get run off the road or shot.

Well, to her, it was a big freakin' deal.

Because nobody messed with her flock.

CHAPTER 5

It was Monday of the Canada Day long weekend, and most businesses were closed, allowing their employees to celebrate the country's big B-Day. Calgary had been besieged by an oppressive heat wave for the last five days; most of the human population had hunkered down to ride it out in the comfort of their air-conditioned homes, while some left town to reconvene with nature at their favorite campsite or cabin.

The King's Army had been out in full force, despite the sweltering heat that remained long past the setting of the sun. They'd been hunting for almost a week, slowly closing in on their targets. Two young brothers, Ollivander and Adrianus, were missing; they were two of the youngest Vampires in existence, and came from the community's wealthiest family.

A week ago, Kye had gotten a phone call from a distraught maid at the Westing estate saying the place had been attacked by Rebels. The King's Warriors had arrived too late to save the head of the household and his mate; their tortured bodies, along with most of the staff, had been left in a pile in the yard for the sun to find.

Keltti had insisted on going with the males that night. It was the most horrific thing she'd ever seen. The victims had known death was coming, had probably even prayed for it. The household staff had been lined up on their knees and shot in the head one by one. They were nothing but collateral damage to the Rebels.

The real targets had been Calveen and Cinthia Westing. They had been trussed to the ceiling with silver chains, their bodies bearing hundreds of slash and stab wounds. Somebody had wanted something from them, badly enough to spend hours carving slice after slice into their bodies. The motives behind the attack were still unclear; the only remaining witnesses were the young males and their housekeeper, Ommi.

She was still recovering at Bloddrikker Castle, having survived the bullet to her face. Keltti had spent time healing her everyday since the attack, and the old females' abrasive attitude was starting to grow on her.

Tonight, the King's Warriors were following a lead and Keltti had insisted on coming along. Ommi's distress at not finding the brothers was increasing by the day, and her anxiety was contagious.

Tor parked the SUV in front of North Ridge Middle School and left the engine running. The streetlight above them shone through his long blond hair, giving it an unearthly glow that contrasted nicely with his leather coat. He caught Keltti's gaze in the rear-view mirror and nodded; it was his way of telling her not to worry, that he'd watch Stu's back. It had taken her a while to understand his cryptic looks, but she was becoming fairly fluent with the serious-looking Vamp's body language.

He got out of the vehicle and Stu turned around in the passenger seat, his intense gaze searing into her. "Stay in the vehicle. If you see anyone but me or Tor, get the hell out of here."

She fought the urge to roll her eyes. It was the same line every time. At the first sign of trouble, she would leave. Yep, she hadn't forgotten since last night. Or the night before. She knew the drill.

His eyes were darker tonight, bordering on red; his broad shoulders tenser than usual. Maybe she wasn't the only one who could feel the weight of the big elephant in the room. Once again, she felt a blush creeping up her cheeks as she tried to keep her thoughts professional. For the last six weeks, Stu had studiously ignored her when she was at the Castle or working in the field with his brothers. She knew he had been trading with the other males to avoid the shifts she would be around for.

What had she done wrong? Her stomach clenched, the sick feeling of embarrassment sliding through her. His intense gaze was still locked on hers, and she refused to be the first to look away. Why did this have to be so awkward?

"Stay safe." she told him, using the same words, in the same calm tone she used with all the soldiers. No hidden meanings, no dishonesty; she really did want him to come back unharmed. All of them—even Stu—had come to mean something to her. They were her flock.

My Vampire Flock, she told herself. Yeah, she was such a dork.

His heated gaze was filled with undecipherable emotions; and she was glad when he didn't say anything.

Tor tapped impatiently on the windshield with the butt of his gun, and Stu exited the SUV with a growl. Keltti immediately climbed across the console into the front seat and locked the doors. Before they disappeared around the corner of the school, Stu looked back and she shot him two thumbs up with a sunny smile that she wasn't really feeling.

He didn't smile back.

The locks at the middle school that were intended to keep vandals out didn't last more than fifteen seconds against Stu and a thin piece of wire. Kye had already shut off the alarm system from the Operations Room at the castle.

"They're here," Stu said, and Tor nodded his agreement; the scent of the young males was fresh.

It didn't take long to search the two floors of the middle school classrooms, until the scent led them downstairs to the gym locker rooms.

The hallway was lit by a green EXIT sign at each end;

the Warriors tread noiselessly across the tile floor towards the boys' change room where they could hear voices.

Simultaneously they holstered their weapons; this was a rescue mission, and they didn't want to scare the boys. Stu made sure to scuff his boots as he entered the change room so that they'd hear his arrival. Tor should have gone first, since his stunningly handsome good looks were less likely to startle the brothers. But, finding reassuring words for their targets would be necessary, and that was something Tor was likely to fuck up. A literary master he was not.

The two males were on the far side of the room. Both stopped in the midst of digging through a box marked LOST & FOUND. They glanced up and froze when they saw Stu standing in the doorway; the smaller one made a little sound of distress and the other one quickly stepped in front of him.

The older one was about six feet tall and handsome, in an aristocratic sort of way, with dark hair tipped with bright blue ends hanging in his face. He had two eyebrow piercings, a stud in his nose, and multiple rings hanging from his right ear. He had obviously made a good run at rebelling against the upper-class circle that he'd been born into.

These were definitely the missing Westing males; Stu recognized their scent from the estate house.

"Ahh…I'm Stukavarius…with the King's Army…" Fuck, why the hell hadn't Sarge sent someone who would know what to say to the terrified brothers? He wasn't good at this talking shit. And Tor was even worse.

The boys stayed motionless, waiting to see how this would play out.

"I'm here to take you to—"

"We're not going anywhere with you." The older brother's voice wobbled with fear, but there was conviction in his words. This wasn't going to go well; the boys didn't trust him worth shit.

Stu moved away from the door, thinking that, maybe if

he took a seat on one of the benches, he'd appear less intimidating. He caught the front of his coat as he bent down, trying to keep the daggers on his chest from their view.

He winced as a loud *bang!* bounced off the tiles, assaulting his sensitive hearing as it echoed around the room. He landed hard on the bench, and pain shot through his back side. *WTF?* He reached around and tugged at his long coat, growling when he saw the hole in it and the blood dripping across the bench.

"Son of a *bitch!*" Stu snarled. The young male across the room stared with wide eyes, a gun still in his shaking hand. "You shot me in the fucking ass!"

He could feel Tor's presence now, standing in the doorway. Gods, he was royally fucking up this whole mission. He lifted his hand to the comm link, slowly so he wouldn't startle the Westling boy and get shot again. "Keltti, we need you. The west doors are unlocked; we're downstairs in the boys' change room."

Silence took over, adding to the smell of fresh blood and sweaty gym socks, making the whole situation that much more awkward. He glanced over his shoulder at Tor and caught a disapproving look from the blond Warrior. Yeah, he knew it was probably a bad idea to bring the Witch into the mix, but he had no idea how else to diffuse the situation—without shooting the little asshole who'd had the balls to shoot him first.

His ass throbbed in time with his heartbeat. The ache was just an annoyance; nothing that he couldn't handle on his own. But, he was selfish and wanted a taste of the soothing vibes that filled the air whenever she was around.

Her light footsteps preceded her before she stepped into the room. Every male in the room looked to her except Tor; his eyes stayed firmly on the gun that was bouncing back and forth between him and Stu.

"Gentlemen?" She took it all in with a sweep of her beautiful green eyes, never letting the calm smile fade from her lips. "Everybody okay?" She moved to step around Tor, and he blocked her entrance into the room. "It's okay," she told him, placing her hand over his wrist and guiding his gun towards the floor. "You can put that away."

Stu couldn't see her face from where he sat, but he knew her eyes would be asking Tor to trust her. Predictably, the Warrior holstered his weapon. Gods, how did she do that without a single word?

Stu watched, unable to look away as she glided over and sat on the bench next to him. She didn't even glance at the youths across the room. Stu could smell their wavering confusion and suspicion in the air.

"What happened?" She gently took his arm in her hands, and he tried not to sigh as her healing magic slid into him.

"Nothing, the bullet just grazed me." He should have been able to deal with it himself, but the frequent feedings at the Blood Daughters' Manor were no longer sustaining his bodies healing abilities. The bloodlust had been getting worse, riding him harder every time he was around the Witch. For six weeks to be exact. Not that he'd ever admit it.

Much too soon for his liking, she released his hand and looked over to where the males were watching her, their fascination obvious. They'd probably never met a Witch before, especially one that could heal. Stu wondered if they could feel the healing energy that threaded its way around the room. Judging by their faces, they probably could.

"I'm Keltti." She gestured to the gun the older brother was holding. "You can put that away. They won't hurt you."

"How do you know they won't?" He sounded afraid, but Stu didn't miss the note of hope in his voice.

"I won't let them."

He glanced behind him to where the younger male was staring at Keltti. "I don't think they're here to hurt us." His voice was tiny in comparison to the other males in the room.

Keltti held out her hand, and the youngster stepped out from behind his older brother to approach her. His light brown hair was cut short, and his stick-thin arms and legs poked out of expensive-looking clothes that were now rumpled and stained from being on the run for a week. The dark shadows under his eyes were probably new, and they were unsettling to see on someone so young. He was about ten years old, and shorter than the Witch he now stood in front of.

"What are you?" he whispered.

"A Witch," she whispered back.

"Cool." His eyes were huge, and he was clearly captivated by the healer's sweet smile. Stu couldn't afford to throw any rocks, not when it came to the Witches charms. Glass houses, and all that bullshit.

"Are you Ollivander?" He nodded. "And this is your brother, Adrianus?" Another nod, and the older male took a step closer.

Keltti looked back at the older brother and held out her hand, looking pointedly at the gun he still held. "I'll hold that for you, Adrian. We wouldn't want any more accidents, would we?" Clever girl, making it sound like the first shot had been an accident; giving him an opportunity for redemption. The bastard had clearly shot him on purpose, but Stu would play along if it meant that they could all get the hell out of here.

He handed it to her, butt first without hesitation, actually looking relieved to be rid of it. His gaze skittered across Stu and quickly back to the little Witch.

She clicked the gun's safety on without looking, and slid it into Stu's hand.

"Are you hungry Ollie?"

He nodded shyly, and said, "Adrian is too, he needs blood."

A blush crept up Adrian's face, and Stu tried not to lose his temper. The older brother had already gone through The Change; he was probably in his early thirties and new enough to the blood-hunger that talking about it to a beautiful woman was embarrassing. The young males had been sheltered their entire lives; their parents had most likely brought in a blood donor for the older one every few weeks.

Keltti stood up and took Ollivander's hand. "I'm hungry too. Let's see what we can find to eat."

The blue-haired male kept stealing glances at Stu's Witch.

Stu's hand strayed to the hilt of his dagger; he didn't like when other males stared at her. He caught the asshat's eyes in the rear-view and felt his own turning red. There was a moment when he held Stu's gaze defiantly, but it didn't last long, and he returned to staring out the window.

In the backseat, Keltti continued her friendly exchange with Ollivander, asking him mundane things that slowly started to put him at ease. He was starting to trust the little Witch, and Stu was impressed with her gentle inquiries that helped gather info on what had really happened at the Westing Estate.

That frightful evening, a group of five Rebels had forced their way past the butler and rounded up everyone in the house at gunpoint. The boys had used a hidden trap door in Adrian's closet that led to an escape tunnel. They had run as far as they could before they took shelter in a garden shed for two days. Hungry and scared, they'd broken into the middle school and had been hiding there ever since. There had been enough canned food in the cafeteria to keep themselves fed and they'd hidden in the gym storage room when the janitors had come to do summer maintenance.

Keltti praised their quick thinking and reassured them that they'd done the smart thing. He didn't envy her when she told them their parents had been murdered. She still had her arms wrapped around the small male, his shoulders shaking as he cried. Her magic stirred peacefully, soothing as it wove its way through the vehicle.

Bloddrikker Castle was well equipped to handle a large number of guests when necessary. There were plenty of lavish suites for those who came voluntarily, and just as many cells for those who did not. However, it was not set up to care for unaccompanied children.

"I'm not just leaving them here! Who's going to take care of them?" Keltti kept her voice low, aware that the Westing males were just around the corner in the kitchen, devouring a plate of sandwiches and veggies that she'd made them. Adrian's hearing would be sensitive enough to hear their conversation if she raised her voice.

"The older one can watch Ollivander, until we find family that will take them in." Captain Vernar was clearly not used to explaining himself, especially to someone who was half the size of a full-grown male Warrior.

"How long will that take? And who knows if we can even trust whoever just shows up for them? Nobody cared enough to even look except for us!" She didn't have to point out that the brothers came with a hefty inheritance. The Westing family had been well known in the supernatural community.

Ollivander came out of the kitchen, stumbling over his own feet in his haste to get to her. She smiled down at him and wiped a smear of mustard off his chin.

"Did you get enough to eat?"

"Yes, thank you." She put her arm around him protectively and gave the Captain one of her best tenacious looks.

"What's going on?" Adrian asked from behind them, obviously picking up on the underlying tension.

"We're just discussing what suite to put you two in for the night." Her not-so-subtle hint was aimed at the Captain. The hard lines around his eyes softened for a second before he gave in and told her to find a room on the third floor that had two beds. He walked away, shaking his head in exasperation.

"Come on guys, I'll take you upstairs."

"Adrianus will come with me." She turned, surprised to see Stu standing in the hallway with them; she was usually hyper-aware of his presence.

The older brother looked at her uneasily. She wasn't sure if he was more worried about leaving his little brother with her, or with being alone with the formidable Warrior.

"Thanks, but I'll take them." She felt Ollie's hand clutching her loose olive-green sweater, and knew the hulking male was scaring both brothers. Couldn't he at least *try* to not be so intimidating?

Stu clapped his huge hand on Adrian's shoulder, while keeping his dark eyes on her. "We need to have a talk; just us males."

Oh boy, that did not sound good. Was he still angry about being shot? Adrian's pale face had lost all it's remaining color, and she felt a maternal streak flare up, turning to anger.

"Not tonight, the boys are tired and need to get some sleep."

"Adrian's *hungry*," Stu said.

What? Oh! Keltti had forgotten that he'd need to feed tonight. And Stu was offering to take him for blood. Goddess, she was an idiot!

"Oh." His eyes roved down to her neck and lingered long enough to make her blush. The knowing look on his face said he was thinking about feeding as well, which automatically brought up images of offering him her vein— which was beyond stupid. She opened her mouth to say something, but nothing came out.

Ollie tugged on her sweater, and she tore her eyes away from the huge male encroaching on her self-preservation so she could give the boy her attention.

"I don't want Adrian to go with *him*." His nervous eyes bounced between her and Stu.

"It's okay, he's going to take Adrian to get some blood." Ollie still didn't look convinced.

"What if he shoots my brother?" He lowered his voice even further, and told her, "He has a gun. I saw it."

Ah, so that was part of the problem; the youngster had

probably never seen a gun until the night the Rebels had attacked. Vampire children were rare, and the brothers most likely had been sheltered from weapons and the war that existed among their kind. He would have a hard time differentiating between a Sterken and a Warrior in the King's Army.

"Stu will protect your brother, I promise. I trust him with my life."

Hope clashed with the fear in his eyes. "Really?"

"Absolutely."

"He's...*scary*."

"Maybe he's hungry too." She stole a glance at the male in question, and yeah, he was staring at her as if he wanted to devour her. Heat pooled in her belly, reminding her that she had hungers of her own—and this Warrior would likely know exactly how to satisfy them.

Turning abruptly, he growled at Adrian, "Lets go."

"Stu?" He looked back and raised an eyebrow questioningly at her.

"You should change before you go." She felt her face heat up even further at his confusion and she slanted her gaze towards his torn pants.

"I can see your bum!" Leave it to the ten-year-old to point out the obvious.

Stu drummed his fingers on the steering wheel.

Sabrina, he thought absently. *Tor calls this one Sabrina.* All the damn SUVs in the fleet were the same identical black, so how the hell was anyone suppose to tell them apart?

He was on edge, mostly from being around the delectable Witch, and partly from finding the boys. It had brought up a whole new line of thinking that he wasn't exactly comfortable with.

The Warriors were getting older, and they'd lost a lot of good males in the last century. The Vampire population was on a slow, steady decline, while humans were reproducing at an exponential rate. The last male born to one of the

Warrior's bloodlines had been Kye. That was almost seventy years ago.

The Rebels were able to add to their ranks by swaying regular Vamp citizens to their way of thinking. There would always be someone unhappy with the current leadership that could be recruited to fight against the Monarchy.

The Westing family had been firm allies of the King. Stu would bet his left nut that the torture Calveen and Cinthia had endured was the Sterkens way of trying to force their allegiance to the Rebels side. And when they wouldn't be converted, they were killed. Their money and influence would have been a huge asset. Ollivander and Adrianus would have been an even bigger bonus; little soldiers for the Sterken to brainwash.

"Where'd you get the gun?"

Adrian flinched in the seat next to him. "Uh, my dad kept it in the escape tunnel. Just in case."

"Did he ever teach you to use it? Take you out to practice at the range?"

"No, last night was my first time."

"So you shot me, the first time you ever pulled the trigger?"

"Ah, yeah, I guess so."

"Were you aiming for my ass?"

"Mmm… not specifically at your… ass, just—like, kinda aiming at you in general."

"I could teach you."

"What?" The kid sounded confused; he probably had been expecting some anger or condemnation from Stu. But he'd been willing to pick up arms in defense of his brother, and he had just as much reason to hate the Rebels as any Warrior. It was far past time that the general Vamp population knew how to protect themselves; nobody was safe from the reaches of the war.

"I'll show you how to use it. If it's your life on the line, you don't want to be shooting anyone in the ass. Shots to the head and the heart, those are what'll keep you alive."

Adrian nodded thoughtfully, and Stu was relieved to let the radio fill the silence.

The young male didn't come from one of the Warrior bloodlines, but there was a hint of a soldier's personality behind the rebellious exterior. With enough nurturing and training, he could be shaped into a fine Warrior.

He wished Keltti could see him now, being all paternal and shit.

"So, ah… Where are we going?"

"The Blood Daughters' Manor." Most of the females he'd fed from had probably come from there; they catered to a variety of clients. Unless the Westing's had kept a Blood Slave. It wasn't unheard of to have a human on the payroll just for that reason.

"Do they have… Witches?"

Stu damn near drove them off the road and he turned to growl at the younger male. "Son, you couldn't handle a Witch." Fuck, *he* could barely handle a Witch—an inexperienced, spoon-fed adolescent like Adrian wouldn't stand a chance.

CHAPTER 6

Ollie had fallen asleep somewhere between chapters two and three of The Witch of Blackbird Pond. Keltti turned off her phone; thank the Goddess for digital eBooks.

The boy had been ecstatic to visit Ommi in the infirmary; she'd been somewhat of a nanny to the Westings, and Keltti was happy to see them reunited. Once the older female had started to look tired, Keltti had prodded Ollie out the door with promises that she'd find some board games to bring for their next visit.

After all the long nights of trying to find the missing males, she was exhausted. She knew she should get up and drive herself back home, but she wanted to make sure Adrian got settled into the guest suite. His bed sat waiting opposite of where she lay next to Ollie. She reclined against a pile of pillows that were cloud-soft, on top of the thick navy duvet that nearly hid the youngster sleeping next to her.

Yeah, she needed to stay to make sure both boys were safely tucked in. That was it. Not because she wanted to see a certain brooding Warrior. No, she wasn't that masochistic. Was she?

Damn it, yeah, she was.

This inescapable infatuation with someone who couldn't even stand to be in the same room as her was the equivalent of the awkward stage humans went through in their teenage years. There were plenty of other males around, Vampire or otherwise, but she just couldn't muster up any interest in pursuing something with anyone but Stu. If she was smart, she'd get back on the dating website that the humans were using.

Her eyelids felt like sandpaper every time she blinked, and they closed without her permission. She'd just rest them for a minute but wouldn't sleep.

Stu had felt a headache brewing since he pulled into the Blood Daughters' Manor parking lot. It had only gotten worse as the night went on. Now that he had finally wrangled Adrian into the SUV, it was a pounding beast, clawing at his skull to escape.

He'd started to feed at the Manor, but...well, shit—he didn't know what the hell was wrong with him. Just a few sips was all he'd been able to manage. There had been plenty of females. And probably even a few males, but he wasn't into that. He wasn't into *any* of it—the blondes, the brunettes, the redheads. None of them were good enough. The only female on his mind was a sweet little Witch that he'd been trying to ignore for the last month and a half.

She'd been the perfect picture of civility; her growing affection and concern for the Warriors' wellbeing was genuine, and she was always polite to him. But he didn't want her polished professional attitude, or her ladylike manners. He wanted the natural infectious laugh she had when Arvid dropped a lame movie quote. And the gentle way she had teased Ros for weeks to get him to the point where he was comfortable joking with her. And the way that she had learned to communicate with Tor with a single gesture of her graceful body. Most of all, he wanted her surrender, the total abandonment of the rules and expectations that kept her so modest and refined.

But he deserved her clinical detachment. He'd been a fucking bonehead, avoiding her because he was scared shitless. His running away had hurt her. When she laughed, the corners of her eyes tightened whenever she caught him looking. He'd caused that pain. He was such a slimeball of a male.

The pain had eventually faded into disappointment and acceptance. And something that looked a lot like shame. Gods, she hadn't done a damn thing wrong. Her remorse ate at him, cutting at his chest like a dull blade and souring the fresh blood that sat in his stomach like a rock.

Stu pulled into the parkade and rode the elevator up to the third floor with Adrian in tow. He could sense her as soon as he stepped out of the lift. She had insisted on going home every morning once she knew her healing gift was no longer needed, and for a second, his heart squeezed with something akin to optimism. But he quickly realized that she was in one of the guest suites, not his room as he'd prematurely assumed.

He didn't need anyone to tell him which apartment she was in—he could already sense her through the door. It was unlocked and he let himself in with Adrian following close on his heels like a lost little puppy. The young male immediately spotted the empty bed across the room and crawled under the covers, his flushed face noticeable in the dark.

Keltti was asleep on her back with her head turned towards Ollivander. They both looked peaceful and content; their matching light-colored hair made her look like a doting mother watching over her young. His heart gave a painful hiccup, and damn, something about that scenario appealed to him on a level he'd never considered before.

He had no idea how long he stood there, letting his mind wander down a road that he'd always thought was off limits to a male like him.

Ollivander stirred under the covers, rolling closer to the Witch and settling back into sleep with a sigh. If he woke and saw Stu standing in the doorway, like some giant fucking boogieman, he'd be terrified; Stu shut the door and gently lowered himself to sit on the mattress next to Keltti.

He'd only allowed himself to touch her three times since the night they met; only when he'd been injured and needed healing. Now he hesitated, not sure what kind of reaction he'd receive if he woke her.

There was only one way to find out.

She sat up as soon as he touched her, her eyes blinking sleepily in the dark. "What—"

"Shhh, you'll wake them," he cautioned.

After several seconds, she seemed to realize where she was and moved to get off the bed. He gave her room, making sure she didn't stumble into anything before they reached the hallway where she had enough light to see again.

"Good night." Her eyes were guarded, her tone dispassionate and something in him snapped, unleashing a churning jumble of emotions that only served to piss him off.

"Where do you think you're going?" He knew he was growling but didn't care.

"Home." She moved toward the elevators but he stepped in front of her, letting the width of his chest get right in her face, invading her personal space, and hoping for a reaction. Anything but her cool disengagement from him.

Her eyebrows rose, and she had to tilt her head back to look him in the eye. "Your eyes are red," she observed softly.

"It happens," he told her flatly. There was no point in reminding her that it was an involuntary reaction to his turbulent emotions. He might as well lay all his cards on the table now. His body was reacting to her nearness; her intoxicating scent invaded his nose while his eyes feasted on the feminine curves beneath her soft sweater and leggings. Her confusion only pissed him off more.

"Oh." She backed up a step, trying to put some distance between them. He easily followed her until her back hit the wall.

"Stu?" Her voice was breathy, reminding him what she would sound like after he kissed her senseless. She could pretend all she wanted; her dilated pupils and racing heart told him just how much she wanted this.

He leaned forward, holding her by the shoulders as he let his body press into hers until she was effectively trapped against the wall. She didn't protest as he closed the distance and brushed his lips against hers.

"Why?" Her whisper was feather-light against his cheek.

"Why, what?" He planted kisses across her jaw and felt her shiver when he started down her neck.

"Why now? Why me? You already went out tonight." She gasped when he pulled back far enough to look her in the eye. A snarl grated through his chest and he knew he was gripping her hard enough to leave bruises.

"There's only one thing I've been craving, and I sure as hell couldn't get it from the Blood Daughters." He waited, wanting to hear her ask so he could be crystal-clear about tonight.

"What are you... craving?" Yeah, she was scared to ask, but Stu was glad she did; he needed her to know.

"You." His hands slid lower, skimming the sides of her breasts as he inhaled that wonderful springtime scent from behind her ear. It was a sheer act of will power to stop himself before his shaking hands could continue downwards. Just a few more scant inches and he'd be able to fill his palms with her perfectly shaped backside. Then it would just be a matter of tilting his hips so that the erection in his leathers could get up close and personal against her sweater.

She blinked up at him and the tentative joy he saw only reminded him of what a jerk he'd been to her. Had she really doubted that any male would want her? He'd been such an idiot to deny her...

But he was still a Warrior in the King's Army. That hadn't changed. And it never would. He couldn't bond with her, but... There were still things they could do without completing the mating bond.

Yeah, sex was off the table, but there was a whole menu of options available for them. And he wasn't feeling real

A Flock of Vampires

picky either—he'd be a-okay with anything at this point. Any damn thing that gave his little Witch some of the pleasure she deserved.

He nuzzled the side of her neck, savoring the small gasp it elicited from her, before drawing his fang across the sensitive skin. Her pulse leapt in response.

His suite was just down the hall and would provide them with more privacy, but he knew if they took this horizontal, nothing would be able to stop him from taking more than he should. No, he had to draw the line at taking her blood—anything more wouldn't be fair to her.

"Stu?" Her soft plea chased away the last of his doubts. Instinct and need overpowered any semblance of rational thought, and he sank his fangs into her waiting neck.

CHAPTER 7

In the last decade or so, Downtown Calgary had undergone several overhauls in an effort to appeal to a new, younger, hipper crowd. Abandoned warehouses had been rejuvenated into fresh funky loft apartments, and most of the older mom-and-pop shops selling anything from sandwiches to jewellery were slowly pushed out of business, leaving Starbucks and Tim Horton's to swoop in and buy up the real estate.

Large columns of concrete, steel, and glass rose above the older brick and mortar buildings, dominating the skyline and blocking the sunlight from the pedestrians on the sidewalk.

The large oil companies were bouncing back from the 2008 recession and doing their best to assure investors and employees alike that everything was hunky-dory. They fought to outdo each other by pouring massive amounts of money into renovating their head offices into gigantic architectural marvels, playing a ridiculous game of one-upmanship. Keltti doubted there would be a winner in their absurd mine-is-bigger-than-yours competition.

There were a number of causalities to the continuous upwards urban sprawl; the homeless being one of them. Calgary's homeless population was mostly human; a large group of people, all finding themselves with dwindling options and their territory shrinking by the day. They were forced into whatever small spaces they could find: in dark alleys, under the Center Street Bridge, or into a cluster of

A Flock of Vampires

trees found in the abundant number of parks where middle-class families played Frisbee and walked their well-groomed dogs during the day.

Those who were smart—and lucky—managed to find an available bed for the night at one of the drop-in shelters. And those who didn't—well, they were the reason for the large surge in the supernatural population. Easy prey who wouldn't be immediately missed was a huge lure for those looking for an uncomplicated meal.

Keltti had gotten to know a number of the drifters; most of whom were already aware of things that weren't entirely human. Word got around here, and those who were sane enough to be wary of the unexplained lived longer.

There was a women and children's emergency shelter for victims of domestic abuse nestled between the Elbow River and Macleod Trail; its location kept private to protect its residents from unannounced visits by their abusers. Last month, the Warriors had rescued a previous tenant from a Soul Eater, returning her to the shelter at her request.

Lacey, the woman who ran the place, had called Keltti's cell today, calmly requesting a visit from the healer.

"Of course. I'll be right there Lacey."

"No, wait until tonight. You should invite *your friends*."

"My friends?"

"You know, the ones that can take care of *unusual problems*."

Keltti realized Lacey must be talking about the King's Warriors but didn't want to say anything in front of whomever she was with.

"I understand, I'm sure they'd be delighted to come too... Do you have an *unusual problem* Lacey?"

"Ahh, yeah... You could say that."

"Are you in danger? Is everyone there safe?" Keltti jumped up, ready to drive over there right then if Lacey was in trouble.

"Yes, yes, we're all okay. We'll be fine until you get here." Her voice was tense but honest, and there were children

63

laughing in the background.

"Okay, I'll see you tonight. Call me if you need me sooner."

"Thanks, Keltti."

After hanging up, she immediately called Kye and arranged for one of the patrols to meet her at Lacey's as soon as sunset came.

Stu guided one of the SUVs, Naiomi, to a stop directly behind Keltti's little grey sedan. She ran lightly down the steps to meet him and Arvid halfway across the yard before they could reach the door. Rain fell lightly around them, masking the sounds of nearby traffic. Little droplets of moisture collected in her hair, reflecting the glow from the streetlights before running off.

"Hey, they're inside. But you guys need to tone it down before you go in."

Stu frowned. "Tone what down?"

"All of *this*." She waved her hand, the gesture encompassing both of the Warriors. "They're nervous around men. And you two look like you're about to go to war with a small country."

Arvid smirked, his perfect white teeth flashing. "I'm as sweet and innocent as cotton candy."

Ketti rolled her eyes. "You're about as innocent as a fox in the henhouse."

Trying to keep the irritation off his face, Stu buttoned his long coat across his chest; he didn't like his weapons so far out of his reach. Concealed was one thing, inaccessible was a whole other case. Inaccessible could get him killed.

Arvid followed suit, thankfully covering up his god-awful T-shirt. The words COUNT BROCCULA were plastered across his chest, over a cartoon broccoli with blood-tipped fangs. His warped sense of humor was disturbing on so many levels.

"Well, on a scale of one-to-ten, your scariness factor has dropped to about thirty-six." Shaking her head, she started back towards the small house. "Stay behind me and try not to look threatening."

Lacey was waiting inside, sitting on an old striped couch next to another woman. Both women held steaming cups of tea, silently watching two young children playing with toys in the corner.

Keltti suspected Lacey had once been a victim of domestic violence herself, but she had never felt it was appropriate to ask. The small woman looked to be in her forties, with short dark brown hair streaked with silver. Her eyes were kind, and she didn't flinch when the Warriors filed into the small living room.

The other woman, Carina, looked up at the males and her eyes widened, her tea sloshing onto the carpet as her hands started to shake. Keltti took a seat on her other side and took the cup from her hands.

"Carina, this is Arvid and Stu—"

"Vampires!" Her whispered accusation was like a gunshot, and even the children stopped what they were doing to look over at their mother.

"I know it's hard to believe, but they're here to help." Keltti took her hand, letting out a trickle of healing energy. Bandages that Lacey had applied before Keltti could get there peeked out of her collar and shirt sleeves. The injuries, jagged Vampires bites, called to her healing gift, but Keltti didn't want to scare the poor woman further by using magic. Finding out Vampires existed was traumatic enough for her; there was no need to throw a Witch into the mix.

Two nights ago, Carina had gone for a walk after putting her kids to bed. Lacey had assumed that she'd fallen into old habits and was holed up somewhere with a little baggie of angel dust and would return in a day or two. Instead of coming back riding a drug comedown, she'd been bleeding from over a dozen bites and hysterically ranting about Vampires. Lacey had done a good job of calming her down, while shielding the children from as much as she could.

"Mama?" the little girl, probably about four years old,

asked timidly.

When Carina didn't answer, Keltti gave the kids a kind smile. "It's okay, my friends are here to find out who hurt your mom."

The tension in the room ratcheted up, making even the unflappable Lacey start to look uneasy.

Abruptly, Arvid glided across the room and carefully took a seat in an old armchair. Keltti cringed, expecting the thin legs on it to give out under his weight. They both let out a relieved breath when he didn't end up crashing to the floor, and he pulled a king-size chocolate bar from his pocket. He studiously ignored the children as they watched him slowly unwrap it and break off a piece. Popping it into his mouth, he bit down, effectively showing everyone perfect white teeth without a trace of fang.

Breaking off another piece, he ate slowly while the kids watched with undisguised envy. They likely didn't get a lot of treats, judging by their thin bodies and rapt expressions.

Splitting the wrapper open even further, he glanced across the coffee table at the youngsters and asked, "Does anybody want some?" Their faces were hopeful while their bodies hesitated, sensing their mother was afraid so they should be too. He placed the bar in the middle of the table and sat back, pinning Keltti with his eyes.

"Oh yeah, I'll have some." She broke off a piece and smiled. "Thanks, Arvid."

He nodded an acknowledgement and pretended not to notice when the little boy crept forward and grabbed the rest of it. Probably six years old, he obviously took his older brother role seriously and brought the treat to his sister to share. Their mother watched the entire exchange without a word, her pale face flustered.

"Carina, do you know where they were holding you?" The woman flinched like she'd been slapped, and Keltti wished there was way to get the information without upsetting her.

"Across the... The cem—cemetery."

"How many were there?"

"Four… I think four. Maybe five."

"How did you get away?"

"They didn't tie me up; they just locked the bedroom door. I kicked the door in. It was flimsy; I knew where to hit it—my ex used to lock us… Never mind. I heard them yelling and coming after me but once I was outside, they didn't follow."

"I'm so glad you were strong enough to get away, Carina."

"I had to get back to my babies." Her voice was still dulled by shock and whatever painkiller Lacey had given her. "They need me."

"They're lucky to have such a brave mother."

Arvid quietly produced another chocolate bar, this time something nutty, unwrapping it and leaving it on the coffee table. The little girl nudged her brother and the big Warrior winked at them.

Keltti glanced to where Stu was mildly waiting by the door, as still as a statue. He nodded, indicating that they had as much info as they needed. She stood and smiled encouragingly at the other females. "You'll be safe here tonight. We're going to find whoever did this and make sure they can't hurt anyone else."

Stepping outside into the cool air, the Warriors followed like big dark shadows in her prereferral as she headed for the SUV. She turned back towards the house and saw both small children waving from the front window, each clutching a package of candies to their chest. Waving back, she turned and gave Arvid an appraising look.

How many treats did he have hidden in that coat? And how was he not six hundred pounds? She had probably put on two pounds tonight just by *looking* at the stuff.

Stu inhaled deeply, letting the scents of the damp night fill him. It was damn hard to concentrate with Keltti hovering behind them, her natural perfume filling the air and distracting him.

The woman, Carina, had been bleeding when she escaped, and he was able to follow her scent back through the cemetery and onto a quiet residential street with small, single-story houses similar to the one they were coming from.

Vampires had long ago learned to blend in; if not for the smell of them coming from a grey and white home, he'd have assumed it had human residents. The yard needed some work, but overall, it was in descent shape.

He still wasn't used to having the Witch out in the field with them. The handful of times she'd been with them, she'd been safely tucked out of harms way, only joining them once the battle was over. He had no idea what was coming tonight. There were four distinct male Vamp scents. Two Warriors against four Rebels wasn't even a real fucking fight, just a nice warm-up. Still, having a female this close to the action was making him twitchy. Even Arvid was feeling it, protectively keeping her body sandwiched between theirs.

The Rebels usually fell under two different columns: column A was the die-hard believers who went down swinging and ended up dead; column B was the despondent working-class citizens who opposed the monarchy but had no idea what to do about it and ended up joining the Rebels for lack of a better option. They could be rounded up without a lot of trouble, and they usually were shipped back to the King in Norway for punishment. Some could be rehabilitated back to law abiding citizens, while others ended up locked away for good. Stu doubted these bastards would fall into column B; they'd already signed their death certificate by snatching a human and feeding off her. If it wasn't consensual, it wasn't allowed in their world.

Arvid had already called for backup, they would lie low until Keltti was stowed away someplace safe. Like fucking New Zealand. That should be far enough away to keep her safe.

Warmth buzzed just beneath the surface of Keltti's skin, starting on the side of her neck and spreading along her shoulder in a lazy caress. It got stronger every time she was close to Stu, and she had to constantly remind herself to give him space when they were in the field. He was scanning the street, his hand lightly resting on the gun at his hip.

The weird buzzing started to prickle, no longer as enjoyable as before.

She didn't know if she was picking up on his edginess, or if he was sensing hers—either way, the night air suddenly felt more suffocating, and her instincts had her reaching for him. He didn't protest when she found his empty hand. Instead, he pulled her closer into the shelter of his body while fully unholstering his gun. He pressed it into her hand and silenced her protests with a look.

"Take it. You know how to use it." Yeah, she did know how, and the weight of it in her hand was reassuring. Just like the feel of his other hand clenched in hers. "Backup will be here soon. Stay here."

"Stay safe." The words seemed inadequate, and she had to force herself to let go of Stu's hand.

The males moved to leave the cover of the vehicle they were crouched behind. She wanted to yell at them, make them take her with them or at least not leave her alone. Every horror movie she'd ever seen ended with a male telling the female to "stay here," and then they'd end up captured or dead. But this wasn't a movie. It was real life, and out here the Warriors knew how to stay alive better than anyone. So she stayed, clinging to the gun until it bit into the skin of her palm.

She watched as they tread quietly towards the white house, each of them continuously scanning the street as they got closer. A high-pitched whistling started, getting louder, and the Warriors must have realized at the same time she did what was coming.

"Get down!" An explosion rocked the ground and the small car closest to Stu lifted six feet into the air before slamming back down on top of a bed of fire. Smoke billowed upwards, silent against the roar of the flames. Arvid was crouching down behind a dark minivan, shooting at the silhouette of a male that filled the doorway of the house. Rounds of bullets flew back and forth, the sounds lost in the crackle of the nearby blaze.

Keltti scanned the street, panic growing in her breast when she couldn't see Stu.

The blast threw Stu several feet. He landed closer to the house, spooned up against the hedge that bordered the neighboring property. The ringing in his ears was louder than the sounds from the ongoing attack, and he'd lost his comm link in the fall.

Turning, he could see Arvid was holding his own against two shooters: one in the doorway, and one in the shattered basement window. Fucking amateurs, who the hell sets up an ambush and then stands in the wide-open, all backlit like a fucking movie star?

He scanned the neighboring properties, searching for the source of the RPG that had taken out the small car— *there*. Half-way up the thick maple tree on the next lot, he could sense another Vampire.

A quick glance across the street to reassure himself Keltti was okay, and he was ghosting across the grass with his daggers in his hands. The bastard in the tree hadn't earned himself a quick death with a bullet. No, this motherfucker was going to bleed just like he'd made Carina bleed. He approached the house behind the tree, using a sturdy looking trellis to gain access to the roof. Thorns from the rose bush below bit into his hands as he climbed.

Once on the roof, he took a running start and leapt out into the empty air; his long coat snapping out behind him like he was fucking Superman. He wondered if the Witch was watching; she'd seen him kick plenty of ass before, but this flying-through-the-air shit was straight out of a comic book. Not that he was trying to impress her. *Riiiight....*

He caught a thick branch and swung himself towards the Vamp who was dressed all in black. His thick boots connected solidly with the male's chest and he let momentum carry him downwards, landing him on the soft carpet of grass next to the startled Rebel.

He rose to his feet, palming his daggers once again. The shocked look he received was quickly replaced by hatred.

"Fuck you! And the King! Fuck—" He never got to finish his hate-filled tirade, as Stu's fist smashed into his face. Teeth and spit and blood sprayed in an arch, and the injured male scuttled backwards on his butt, trying to get away from the Warrior. Stu matched his pace, a hunter playing with his prey.

The launcher that had been clutched to his chest suddenly came up, pointed at the Warrior. He fumbled with the trigger and Stu tackled him, rolling across the grass while trying to keep the thing from going off in his face. The Rebel was a better fighter than Stu would have expected, and he managed to get in a good kidney-shot.

"Son of a bitch!" Stu grunted and his grip on the Rebel's wrist loosened. The other male took advantage of the distraction and pulled the trigger, a puff of smoke filling the space between them as the recoil slammed them apart.

"Heads up!" Stu yelled, frantically trying to track the projectile as it sailed upwards against the dark sky, before gracefully swan diving back down towards the residential street where dozens of humans were sleeping, unaware of the danger. He cocked back his fist and crushed the Rebels throat in one smooth motion, already running by the time the body hit the ground.

The pricks were really stepping up their game; where the hell had they got an RPG?

The falling rocket whistled merrily as it randomly sought out a target. Stu followed its trajectory and realized with horror it was getting closer to where he'd left the Witch.

"Keltti, *run!*" he bellowed, hoping to the Gods that he'd get to her before the missile landed. Her beautiful green eyes met his, and then she was running. His damn male ego inflated; he liked the fact that she was running *towards* him instead of away.

The RPG landed, a direct hit to the monstrosity of a tree next to where she had been standing seconds before. It blew apart, its multiple trunks splitting and falling in different directions as if it had been hit by lightning. One of the massive limbs crashed down on the vehicle that they'd used for cover earlier; its alarm started shrieking, adding to the mass of chaotic noise. Another large column of wood tipped towards the street, leaning into the power line above their heads. It snapped, sending a cascade of sparks bouncing onto the asphalt. The tower of wood teetered before succumbing to gravity and falling.

"Keltti!" Dread filled his veins as he watched her sprint towards him.

Branches cracked and broke off as the weight of the trunk crashed onto the road; narrowly missing her. A large, twisted branch, still attached to the tree, struck her in the back of the leg as it landed. She went down with a scream, trapped beneath the gnarled bark, as smaller branches of leaves landed around her, hiding her from Stu's view.

Pushing his way through the foliage, he found her lying face down on the cracked road, unconscious. The branch pinning her leg was as wide as his bicep, and he put his full Vampire strength into lifting it. Dozens of smaller branches extended from it, weighing it down, along with the massive trunk it was still attached to. His muscles flexed and popped as he strained to get the fucking thing to move.

Then, Arvid was there, thank the Gods, tugging Keltti out from under the branch. Stu let it go with a groan, sweat running into his eyes as he knelt and cautiously turned her over. Her face had been scraped, and her forehead was starting to swell with a large lump where she'd hit the road; the same road rash covered the palms of her hands. Her leggings hid her injured leg, but Stu didn't smell any blood, so her injury must have been to the bone or muscles.

A black SUV slid to a stop next to them; backup had finally arrived, thank the Gods. Tor jumped out of the passenger seat and held the back door open, while Stu carefully gathered Keltti's limp body into his arms before climbing into the back seat.

"Is she breathing?" Kye asked from the drivers' seat. The vehicle lurched forward as he floored it.

"Yeah, she's breathing."

"What happened?"

"Rebels. They ambushed us. The RPG went off and hit the tree next to her." He smoothed Keltti's hair back from her face, avoiding the bump. "She's cold; really cold."

"You've got to warm her up." He sat there stupidly wondering how he was supposed to do that until Kye yelled at him. "Stu! She needs to warm up *now*. There's a blanket under your seat."

Knowing the other Warrior was right, he reached down and tugged out the grey fabric, trying not to jostle the female in his arms. He tucked the ends underneath her, hoping it would trap any of the body heat she had left. He stayed quiet so Kye could focus on driving while he concentrated on the rise and fall of his Witch's shallow breathing.

CHAPTER 8

Why the fuck didn't they have another healer at the castle?
He wasn't a fucking doctor; he had no idea what to do with
the unconscious bundle in his arms. Head to the infirmary?
No, there was nothing there but a gurney and some tools to
patch a male up when he was bleeding out. The hospital?
Not without them realizing she wasn't human. Fuck, he
didn't know a thing about Witches. Vamps, sure. Humans,
a bit. But not Witches. Gods, he wished he had taken the
time to learn.

First things first; he needed to warm her up.

Taking the stairs at a run, he took her to his suite and
straight into the bathroom. He spun the hot tap as far as it
would go and half as much for the cold. He briefly
considered leaving her clothes on, but knew that he'd need
to get a good look at her leg. Taking a dagger, he slid it up
the outside of her legging, splitting the fabric up past the
knee.

Fuck—it was broken. He could see where the edges of
the bones were fractured and didn't line up perfectly. It was
swollen and bruised, but it didn't look as bad as her head.
He pulled out his cell and dialed Sarge's number.

"Keltti's hurt. I need someone to help me splint her leg.
I'm in my room." Not bothering to wait for a reply, he hung
up.

The tub hadn't finished filling, but he shut it off anyway.
The hot water would only cause more swelling, so he'd have
to warm her up the old-fashioned way. Damn, he was a

74

lucky bastard.

Entering his bedroom, he quickly turned down the covers with one hand and laid her still body on the dark sheets. And didn't that just conjure up a head full of graphic images.

Trying not to think about the many times he'd fantasized about having her in his bed, he methodically removed her shirt and leggings. The bra and panties made him pause, but he reminded himself that clothing would only interfere. He made short work of them and covered her up to her chin in the thick duvet. His boots and weapons took longer than he liked to remove, and his clothes quickly followed.

The mattress dipped as he slid under the covers, shifting with his weight as he settled as close to her as physically possible. He pulled every inch of her slight frame up against his body, turning her so he could hold her from behind. The delicate swell of her ass fit perfectly against his groin. He felt his erection surge to life—and thank fuck, Sarge walked in before he could get lost in that particular train of thought. Kye was close on his heels, carrying a splint and first aid kit.

They both had plenty of experience with bracing broken bones, so logically he knew she was in good hands; but the primitive male instincts that had been brought out by the unfinished mating insisted that no fucking way were these males going to touch her. No. Fucking. Way.

He felt his fangs drop as he growled.

"Whoa, Stu. I'm just going to…" Kye dropped the edge of the blanket and backed off.

"We need to set the bone. Now." Sarge was right, but damn if Stu wanted any other male touching her. He should be the one to do it, to set things right so she could heal. But she was in shock and needed his body heat, and there wasn't a snowball's chance in hell that he would let someone else do that for her. So, fuck—yeah, he needed their help. His arms tightened around her, and he breathed in some of that wonderful fresh sunshine scent as he fought for a calm he wasn't feeling.

"Do it."

Keltti dreamt, the images fading into each other in vivid splashes of color and sound.

Deep green leaves against a midnight sky, rustling in the cool breeze. Happy from the earlier rain, patiently waiting as the world turned closer to the sunlight. Trusting, knowing it would happen. Angry flames so bright that her eyes hurt, burning wood and gunpowder. Shadows wrestling, blood mingling with the wet grass. Her name torn from lips… Lips that tasted wild and desperate…

Pain, blinding and absolute, crushing her. Bright light sliding past, too fast to catch.

Then the warmth and scent of a male surrounded her— Stu. Always Stu. She couldn't shut her eyes without him invading her dreams. She tried to struggle free but heat swamped her, melting her into the sheets as a deep voice murmured, "Sleep, Sunshine. Just sleep."

She was naked. And hungry. And her head hurt. And this wasn't her bed.

Her mind struggled to sort through information as the facts assaulted her. She tried to figure out which ones were relevant and which ones weren't.

Being naked and in someone else's bed—that was definitely important. It would have been worrisome if she hadn't already recognized the clean spicy scent of Stu. She reached over to find an empty expanse of soft sheets that were still warm, as if someone had been lying there a minute ago but had gotten up and left.

Her naïve heart gave a sharp little squeeze in her chest. If she was naked in his bed, what did that mean?

Ros stepped into the bedroom, carrying a steaming bowl that smelled wonderful.

"Hey, how are you feeling?" She stopped herself from sitting up; no need to flash the poor guy for bringing her some food.

"Okay. Good, actually." After a brief bout of small talk that made her headache worse, he left the soup on the nightstand next to a pile of clothes, and left.

After eating and taking inventory of her injuries with a critical eye, she did her best to stay awake, hoping that Stu would come back.

He didn't.

Witches were social creatures; typically living together in covens that filled the need for family. Most never married, preferring to be in the company of their own kind. Once the biological ticking of their clock started counting down, they sought out a male—usually human—until conception occurred, then they returned home. The resulting baby was always a girl, and always carried the Witch's genes.

This undeniable attraction that Keltti felt for Stu had been a calamity of her own making. She'd been without the companionship of a coven for too long, and her body was ready to start her own branch of the family tree.

That had to be it: simple biology.

It was past time for her to do something to fix this nagging loneliness before it ended up swallowing her whole.

Don't think about him.

Her nipples hardened under the thin silk nightgown that she wore, and desire filled her belly and slid lower. Just the thought of him made her skin flush.

She was such an idiot, pining for a male who didn't want her. He'd remained MIA for the remainder of her stay at Bloddrikker Castle, and eventually she'd gotten strong enough to go home by herself.

She needed to get away from here; to be where she could find harmony in her life again. The coven that she had called home in Colorado would welcome her back with open arms. She had good memories there; she'd been a part of the laughter and peace that made it a home. But she wasn't ready to face the pitying looks again, not since the death of her mother.

No, she needed to find somewhere new. Someplace that would welcome a novice Witch; someplace she could learn and grow into the woman she knew she was meant to be. Someplace far away from Stu.

The rain poured from the sky in biblical amounts. Like Stu should be standing on a fucking ark, instead of in the dark shadow of an elm tree with his boots sinking into the dirt between rows of geraniums and daisies.

Across the yard Keltti's cheerful little house watched him, the windows glowing with warm friendly light. He could see her through the set of French-doors as she neatly folded clothes into three suitcases that were lined up on the bed. He should tell her to keep her curtains shut when it was dark out; but then again, who else was going to be creeping around her backyard like some fucking stalker? Yeah, only one bastard that he knew of.

He shouldn't be here tonight. He hadn't seen her since the night she was injured—well, *technically* he'd seen her, if skulking around her property counted like some sort of cordial afternoon tea party.

Sarge had dropped one motherfucker of a bombshell, informing the Warriors that she wasn't coming back. Not just while she was injured, but, like *ever*. Okay, maybe Stu was reading too much into it—Sarge hadn't actually said *never coming back*. But it sure as hell felt like it. And seeing her pack her bags… Fuck, he wanted to go in there and stop her. Pull some meaningful words out of his ass that would match the burning in his chest. Find out if maybe she'd settle for a schmuck like him.

But he couldn't. Wouldn't do it. He had to let her go. He was the reason she still had the little limp as she shuffled back and forth to the closet. There was no way in hell he was going to put her at risk again. And that's exactly what would end up happening to a female mated to a Warrior. She'd constantly be at risk; always a target of the Rebels or anyone else that he pissed off. And he was damn good at pissing others off.

He didn't know where she was going, but it probably wouldn't be hard to find out. Did he really want to know? Fuck, he should just cut this off now, before it got any worse.

Anytime now… Yet he was still here, the icy rain dripping down his neck and soaking into his clothes beneath his coat. And she was still in there, stacking her things into the bags tetris-style, not even aware that tucked in amongst the socks and sweaters, she had a stowaway; because somewhere along the way she'd managed to capture his heart. And now that she had it, it would go wherever she did. Metaphorically of course, since the big lump of muscle and flesh was still thumping away in his chest; but for all intents and purposes it was hers.

Letting the grief and sorrow dance under his skin, he gave up pretending he was hunky-dory with letting her go. He was so *not* fucking okay with this shit. But he had to be. Or, at least, he had to pretend he was.

He turned and walked away.

CHAPTER 9

Five Years Later

Clouds of fallen leaves the color of pale fire swirled through the crisp air; fall had come early to the Rocky Mountains.

Keltti opened the front door of her home to welcome her fourth and final client of the day to her new home-based business, The Healing Grove.

Her client, a small, dark-skinned woman with her ebony hair pulled into a tight bun at the top of her head, was dressed in tight, worn jeans that were paired with a pale grey sweater that hung to mid-thigh. She'd topped off the chic outfit with tall black boots with even taller heels. The female glided up the cracked sidewalk with the gracefulness of a dancer. Or a predator.

"Please come in. I'm Keltti."

"Ka-Shawn," the woman introduced herself. "Thanks for getting me in."

"You're welcome. My office is this way."

Once they were seated in Keltti's second bedroom that had recently been converted to an office, she started with the basics: Height, weight, age, medical history, and so on.

"What can I help you with Ka-Shawn?" She pushed her keyboard away and leaned forward in her chair; there would be time later for entering all the pertinent information into the laptop, for now she wanted to give the young woman her full attention.

Ka-Shawn sighed and looked out the window. "I've

been tired; like really tired. I sleep all night and it's just not enough." She held up her hand and flexed her long fingers. "My nails are breaking. That's not normal. Nothing about me feels normal."

A small shot of alarm wound through Keltti; the bones, nails and teeth of a Werewolf were harder than steel. Something was indeed wrong with this young Wolf. And now that she was truly looking, she could see a dullness to the hair and skin that should have been glowing.

"Has this ever happened before?"

"Nope."

"How long has it been going on?"

"A couple months. And it's getting worse…"

Keltti could tell there was more, something Ka-Shawn wasn't saying. "What is it? You can tell me anything. Total patient/healer confidentiality here. I can't help you if I don't know what's going on." She leaned back in her chair and let the silence settle over the room like a comforting blanket. Pushing for an answer would only make her patient more reluctant to share.

"Last week… I couldn't shift." Her voice was thick with shame and unshed tears. The very thing that twined her two halves together, that bridged the gap between the woman and the wolf, the most essential part of her nature, was broken.

How awful; she must be devastated.

Keltti held out both hands in silent invitation for Ka-Shawn to take. After a moments hesitation their fingers met and Keltti's second sight flared to life. Her vision filled with colors that only she could see. The aura around the Werewolf danced and crackled like a living halo. The bright yellow that denoted all Shifters was muted to a paler version. There were a variety of pinks obvious, showing strong fertility. Subtle greens that faded to grey showed the taint of grief and embarrassment. Those were most likely new, brought on by the inability to shift.

Calling on the light inside herself, she extended a streak

of healing warmth through her fingertips into Ka-Shawns body. Following Keltti's directions, it wound itself through her patient, soaking into everything it touched. It offered a healing boost to every tired cell that felt far too worn for such a young female.

Keltti pushed deeper with the light, reaching past the physical structures of bone and muscle until she found the place where the wolf resided. The beautiful, shimmering source of power nestled at the very center of Ka-Shawn's being was surrounded by a light, gossamer-thin, dark purple webbing. Behind it, the wolf was trapped, pacing and restless. It wanted out and was angry that it couldn't break free.

Her healing light recoiled when it brushed up against the purple strings; they were sticky like spider webs, trying to cling to the light. They resisted any of the healing that she pushed at them.

Surprised at what she'd found, Keltti pulled away from Ka-Shawn and opened her eyes. The young female looked better than when she'd arrived; her hair was glossier, her skin slightly flushed and the tight lines around her eyes were gone.

"Wow, what did you do?" The shock in her voice made Keltti smile absently while she mulled over what she'd seen. It was unlike anything she'd ever encountered before. Looking closer at the aura shining around Ka-Shawn, she realized the tiny indigo strings were barely visible there too. They crawled over the streaks of colour, clinging to the woman like a virus.

Mentally flipping through her healing knowledge, Keltti quickly grasped at possibilities and just as quickly rejected them. Viruses and bacteria bulldozed their way through a victim, this was far more delicate. It was too widespread to be an injury, either physical or supernatural. This was something far different.

A spell perhaps? Witches like Keltti were born with the healing ability, and this had the same subtle flavour—only in a much more twisted, tainted sort of way.

"I healed some of the damage, but it's not a cure. I have an idea of what's going on, but I'll need to do some research to find out for sure." The spell, if that's what it was, was strong and would regularly need power—more power than it was sucking from its host. Who, or what, was feeding it?

"I think it's a spell. A dark spell. It's completely surrounded your wolf."

"What?!" Ka-Shawn's face paled in shock. "How is that possible? How do I fix it?"

"You need to cut off it's source of power and it should fade on its own." Tapping her fingers thoughtfully, Keltti realized it would take someone with the second sight to find the Witch who had cast the original spell. "Are there any Witches at your den?"

"None." Keltti ignored the hint of disfavour; Werewolves were incredibly territorial and didn't have many visitors outside their species. It wasn't personal.

After spending the last five years in Iceland learning from some of the world's oldest and wisest Witches, she was confident she would be able to pick up on any lingering energy left behind from such a dark spell. Getting access to the Werewolf's den would be the first place to start.

After a heated phone call to her brother, Ka-Shawn announced that Keltti was welcome for a *brief* visit at Vollmund Hull. Trying not to eavesdrop, Keltti had made herself busy entering data into her laptop. Still, she had picked up a few tidbits of information that fascinated her.

All Packs were organized into a hierarchy of sorts. Ka-Shawn seemed to be fairly high up, and at the top of the metaphysical totem pole was none other than her brother, Simon.

So, she's the big bad Alpha Wolf's little sister…. Has that made her a target? Keltti intended to find out.

Two days after Keltti had returned to Calgary, Captain Vernar had once again offered her a position working for the King's Army as their official healer. It was merely a formality; her hiatus from their ranks had only been temporary. Unofficially, of course. She hadn't guaranteed her return, but Stu knew she'd been emailing Kye regularly while she was gone. Not that it bothered him—not one fucking bit. She'd consulted on the new infirmary that had been added to Bloddrikker Castle, sending suggestions and recommendations throughout the design and construction phases.

Stu had had the opportunity to see firsthand the new underground facility when Arvid had dug shrapnel out of the back of his arm. It was well laid out and meticulously organized, and even the pale, earth-toned walls reminded him of his Witch.

Not my Witch.

Right, because he hadn't claimed her. Five damn years later, he should be able to keep that shit straight in his head.

He'd known the day she returned, had sensed something was different, even if he didn't know at the time what it was. The cold hard lines of the city had suddenly shifted to become softer, more vibrant with the lives it held. Like a well tended fire with a thick wool blanket to compliment it, the night became more endurable.

And like a junkie, he'd waited as patiently as a male could wait for his next hit of a drug that was, by all means, off limits to him. So, after two weeks of getting settled back into her Bridgeland home, she was back at Bloddrikker. And where the fuck was he? Hiding in his room like a pussy.

The sun had set hours ago; he'd head out with Ros in another thirty minutes. He'd checked and rechecked his weaponry. His daggers were freshly cleaned and sharpened. He'd even replaced the worn laces in his boots. Nothing left to do but head downstairs for the Ops room.

She'd be there.

Someone had bought a bouquet of fresh flowers in earlier; some unnatural blue and orange things suffocating in greenery and a plastic sleeve. He had damn near ripped everyone in the room a new asshole before stuffing the offending gift in the garbage.

What the fuck had those idiots been thinking? She was *a Witch*. She wouldn't want some half-dead weed with fabricated colors that had been concocted in a lab, which would wither and fade on her kitchen table.

As soon at the sun had set, he had headed into the woods behind the castle and dug up a small scraggly pine tree. It was only about eight inches tall, and it had had the misfortune of making a home between two other larger trees that were slowly robbing it of sunlight. It was pitiful and probably a lost cause; and exactly what she wouldn't be able to say no to.

The analogy wasn't lost on him.

Finding himself out of excuses, he took the stairs down to the main floor. Her laughter greeted him before he even got to the Operations room.

Sarge was leaning against one of the tables, his arms crossed casually across his chest. Arvid was standing next to Keltti, a grin on his face; sporting a stupid shirt with an ugly hairy monkey wearing heavy make-up and pearls with the word SASSYQUATCH in bold letters. Kye sat in his usual chair, his ankle resting on his opposite knee while he slowly rocked back and forth. Rostell and Adrian laughed at something she said and he understood why. Keltti's laugh was infectious, and he fought the urge to smile too. He hadn't earned that right.

The small tree sat in the mixing bowl he'd planted it in on the large conference table. It looked even more sickly and pathetic than he remembered, and he hoped the others hadn't told her it was his idea.

"Let me see it," she told Adrian.

With a chagrined smile, he turned his back to her and lifted his shirt. She sucked in her breath and tisked, directing her eyes at Ros. "You did that?"

"Yes ma'am, I did." He didn't sound the least bit sorry.

"With a *sword*?"

"A *wooden* sword."

Stu realized they must be talking about Adrian's training session that afternoon. Ros must've nailed him during practice, and he was showing off the results for Keltti. If he was hoping for sympathy, he was out of luck.

"You should teach him how to duck before moving on to sword-fighting."

The rumble of male laughter continued as they good-naturedly ribbed Adrian about his training.

Keltti glanced up to where Stu was standing in the doorway. Every single thought left him, and whatever greeting he'd planned disappeared.

Her hair was longer, the waves reaching past her should-blades; it looked lighter, like she'd spent some time in the sun while she'd been gone. Eyes, exactly as he remembered them, the same light green of fresh growth in springtime, met his with recognition. And then she smiled. It hit him right in the thorax like a sucker-punch, and he might've taken a step back. He hoped not.

The long skirt and blouse she wore were too pretty for working in the field. Relief and disappointment collided in his head. He knew it would be a bad idea to take her with him; distractions could be deadly in a combat situation. They'd both be safer if she stayed at the castle tonight. But it was a selfish thought, and it didn't take into account the possibility that her healing might be needed by one of the other Warriors.

"...Hey..." *Real smooth, dumbass.* Gods, where was a fucking Soul Eater when he needed one? The longer he stood under her knowing gaze, the more he wished for something to kill with his bare hands so he wouldn't have to produce a semblance of coherent thought.

"*Keltti!*" Ollivander barrelled around the corner, careening into Stu's back and bouncing off like he'd hit a brick wall. The joy on his face faltered, dissolving into the usual mask of unease that he wore around Stu. He rubbed his nose; it wasn't bleeding from the impact but it probably hurt like a son of a bitch, and Stu tried not to smirk.

Giving the Warrior a wide berth, he once again headed for the Witch, where she was waiting to embrace him with open arms and a smile that truly reached her eyes. Not all that different from the tame one she'd given Stu, but he noticed all the same.

"I *missed* you." The male was taller than she was now, and she cradled his head on her shoulder. He was still stick-thin, his arms and legs gangly in a way that made him look like a marionette doll next to her curves.

"I told you I'd come back." Nobody seemed to see the thin sheen of tears in her eyes; she'd obviously missed the young male. After a few seconds of clinging to each other, she stepped back and looked him over. "Look how much you've grown." Her face was all maternal pride, with a touch of sadness that she'd missed his journey from child to teen.

"Are you staying? Ommi said you'd stay." He was serious now, and Stu could see several of the Warriors leaning forward to hear her answer.

"I'm staying." He didn't realize he'd been holding his breath until it left him in a rush. The relief he felt was staggering and something he had no right to feel. At least he could satisfy one of his male urges now—the need to protect her was something that could be carried out without her knowledge. He was damn good at being invisible, and it wouldn't be hard to keep an eye on her when she wasn't with one of his brothers. That is, if she kept to the same nocturnal schedule that she'd adopted when she was working with them five years ago.

Ros shrugged on his long coat and saved Stu from any further awkward non-conversation. "We should get going."

Not trusting his mouth to come up with anything brilliant to say, Stu just nodded and followed Ros out of the room. He could still hear Ollivanders voice, rough from adolescence, but nowhere near the deep bass of a full-grown males.

"Come on, I'll show you the new infirmary. I helped with the construction and painting." Stu was too far away to hear her reply, and he hoped she was telling the youth where he could shove it. Somehow, he doubted it. She was probably already praising him on a job well done.

It took Keltti longer than she planned to extract herself from Bloddrikker Castle.

Ollie and Adrian had followed her to the new infirmary. Ollie rapidly fired questions at her, while Adrian stood quietly off to the side. A quick peek at his aura had confirmed what she'd suspected: he was hurt, most likely by her leaving. She waited until his younger brother was occupied by spinning in an office chair before hugging the older male.

"I'm sorry I left." His body was stiff, and he didn't move at first. Hesitantly, he put his arms around her and she felt his muscles start to loosen. He'd put on a lot of muscle while she'd been gone, and by human standards he looked to be a fully grown adult. By Vamp standards, he was barely out of adolescence, yet he still towered over her.

He didn't say anything, but she felt him nod. It would take time to completely fix whatever trust of his she had broken, but that was fine. Witches and Vampires had long lifespans.

After visiting Ommi in the kitchen, where she was efficiently putting together a buffet fitting of a King, Keltti said her goodbyes and reassured the Westing males that she'd be back the next night. She was glad to see that the older female had found a home at Bloddrikker. The entire castle had a new, well cared for vibe, and even the Warriors had grown to appreciate the surly housekeeper.

The older female looked to be in her sixties by human standards, but she was probably much older. Once her mate had died, she had lost the youthful look all Vamps had. It was rare for a mate to survive when their loved one passed on. Her long silver hair and wrinkles were beautiful, a physical reminder of the strength that she possessed to keep living. She had the hardened heart of a soldier and Keltti was impressed by the loyalty and affection she'd earned from the Westing boys.

She'd lost an eye during the attack and wore an eye patch that somehow matched the bold floral print dresses she preferred from an era long gone, an era before Keltti had even been born.

Making sure her new plant, a small pine sapling, was safely strapped into the passenger seat, Keltti pulled out of the Castle parkade.

"I have a nice terra cotta planter at home for you," she told it. The poor thing was living in a mixing bowl without any drainage that would eventually start to rust. Still, she was touched that the males had thought to welcome her back with the little tree. It was a sweet gesture.

This evening had gone better than she had hoped. Stu had seemed indifferent, yet slightly awkward towards her. Would it always be like this between them? Her dating knowledge was still woefully small; she had neither the time nor the inclination to try dating in Iceland. Hopefully it would become easier to be around him. Her rebellious body had recognized him as soon as he'd stepped in the room. Desire had flooded her, making her heart race and her knees weak. Goddess, she wished she knew why he had such a powerful effect on her. Time had done nothing to diminish the feelings that she'd spent five years trying to ignore.

She turned onto the highway going west and tried to forget about the sexy Vampire she'd left behind.

CHAPTER 10

Vollmund Hull was built on the edge of the Rocky Mountains. The remote location had been home to the Dark Shadow Pack for over two hundred years, long before the first human or Vampire settlers arrived. Their isolation was self-imposed; Wolf Shifters had very little desire to mingle with anyone outside their clan.

Keltti wasn't sure what to expect when she arrived. The compound was built into the side of the mountain and looked to be several stories high. Open windows were carved into the rock face, along with a few doorways that had walkways between them. It managed to look ancient and modern all at once.

She pulled onto the gravel shoulder next to the road, and Ka-Shawn met her at the front door with two other males.

"Keltti, I'm glad you could come." Her greeting sounded genuine, but the faces of the males were anything but friendly. "This is Gregory and Handell. Boys, this is Keltti."

The males, both tall and muscular, had the same dangerous demeanour of a soldier. Their protective stances on either side of Ka-Shawn managed to be intimidating while remaining aloof. Both were definitely guarding the female. They nodded a greeting towards Keltti.

"Welcome to Vollmund Hull. I'll give you a tour." Keltti followed her though the double-wide door into the foyer. The floor was beautifully tiled with white marble, delicately veined with silver and black. The walls were the original stone of the mountain, carved into intricate scenes of a stunning woman reaching for the moon. On another wall, the same woman was surrounded by wolves all watching her with clear reverence in their eyes. The detail was extraordinary, and Keltti would have liked to linger for a closer look. Instead, she did her best to keep up with Ka-Shawn as the small female led her down one hallway after another, pointing out the common rooms along the way.

"This is my room." The door was a thick mahogany wood and opened on silent hinges. There was no window. A crystal chandelier hung from the ceiling, spilling a generous amount of light around the room.

Piles of clothes littered the floor, while CDs and make-up cases covered every available horizontal surface. The unmade bed was covered in deep purple bedding with silver throw pillows. Plastic glow-in-the-dark stars were hung from the ceiling, and posters for music bands that Keltti had never heard of covered the walls.

"So, what are you looking for?" Ka-Shawn pulled her cardigan tighter around her body and shivered.

"Honestly, I have no idea. I'll know it once I see it." Keltti resisted the urge to sugar coat the truth; false promises would always lead to disappointment. Some sort of charm or spell were possibilities, but she was keeping an open mind.

Handell had followed the females into the bedroom and waited silently, leaning against the open doorframe, radiating impatience and skepticism. Aware that she had an audience, she worked quickly. Her second sight offered no help; there was nothing magical about anything in the room.

"Can I see where you eat? And where the food is prepared?" Whatever was affecting Ka-Shawn had to be close enough that she'd come in contact with it regularly.

"Sure, the dining room and kitchen are downstairs."

Keltti stepped out into the hallway and smacked right into someone; another male Shifter, by the feel of the hard chest that she automatically grabbed onto to keep her balance. She had to take a step back so she could look up at his face. He looked as stunned as she felt, and she couldn't help but notice how the hard-chiseled lines of his face were beautiful and masculine all at once. His skin was the color of fresh coffee beans, and just as exotic.

"Sorry, I wasn't watching…" Her thoughts trailed off as he chuckled, the sound coming from low in his throat.

"Nor was I. You must be Keltti; my sister told me you were coming today." He captured her hand in his and energy prickled across her skin. It wasn't entirely unpleasant; it felt like little fingers of static electricity crawling across her palm. "I'm Simon, Alpha of the Dark Shadow Pack."

"Thank you for having me, Alpha." She blushed, and wished she'd phrased that differently.

"Call me Simon." His knowing smile slipped into one more professional as Ka-Shawn inserted herself into the conversation.

"We're going to check out the dining room. Want to tag along?"

"Of course, we don't have visitors often enough for me to pass up the opportunity." Keltti wasn't disillusioned enough to think that the Alpha wanted to spend time getting to know her. No, she was an intruder in his territory, and he wanted to make sure she behaved while she was here. That was fine; she was here to find out what was ailing his sister, not to make new friends.

Vollmund Hull had a surprising amount of activity going on at three in the morning. Shifters passed them on nightly errands, giving Keltti curious glances as they passed, but never stopping to talk. Most likely because of their Alpha's presence, but she didn't sense any precise dislike of her kind.

After checking the kitchen, dining room, supply pantry, workout room, library, and multiple common rooms, Keltti was no closer to helping her patient. There were a number of rooms that were off-limits, but Ka-Shawn assured her they were just personal quarters and the weapons room.

Gregory and Handell hung back from the females, probably having realized she wasn't here to murder the

Alpha's sister. Ka-Shawn kept pace, while Keltti absently retraced their steps until she found herself on one of the outdoor walkways.

She stopped and leaned against the stone railing while her eyes sought out the canopy of stars that were familiar, yet somehow brand new after her time away. Along with the comfort of observing the expected, she allowed her body to relax as the scents and sounds of the outdoors washed over her.

Most immortals (aside from Vampires, but that was probably from their profound fear of sunlight) found balance in nature. Her breathing slowed and her muscles released the tension she'd been holding. Time slowed as she found her inner calm; the energy from the Earth, ancient and nurturing, surrounded her. Her healing gifts made her especially sensitive to the flow of life that encompassed all living things.

This is where she went when she needed to clear her mind—

"Where else do you go? When you want to be alone, to recover from all of this?" She gestured with her hand to encompass what she hoped was the entire compound. "From them?" She pointed at their security entourage.

"Gregory and Handell?" Confusion colored the Shifter's words and deepened the fine lines around her eyes.

"No, males in general. All the testosterone filled caveman junk they try to pull with us. How do you cope with all the macho pigheadedness that comes with the Y chromosome?"

"Ah—I see what you're getting at. I run."

"Where?" She doubted the female used a treadmill. Or even ran on two legs.

Ka-Shawn gestured grandly at the hundreds of acres of woods surrounding them. "Out there."

Keltti looked down at her flats and belatedly wished she'd worn hiking boots.

The bugs weren't usually bad at night, and tonight was no exception. It was a small blessing she knew she should be grateful for.

The Wolves had found a suitable pair of running shoes for her to borrow; another blessing, she acknowledged. Her shirt stubbornly stuck to the sweat on her back, and she felt like she'd been walking for hours. Realistically it had probably only been about forty minutes, but time felt like it was crawling. Or, it felt like time was slogging through a heavily wooded landscape. Just like she currently was.

Simon had insisted on coming along for their wilderness adventure, while his second in command had insisted on a security detail. The female's quiet midnight stroll quickly snowballed into a party of seven. It seemed like overkill to Keltti, but who was she to judge? She had no doubt that the Warriors she worked with would have done the same thing.

The cloudless sky helped her find her way around the low-hanging branches and fallen logs since she didn't have enhanced night vision as the Wolves did. A rock hidden among the dead leaves caught the toe of her shoe, and she pitched forward with a squeal. Simon, the only male Shifter who wasn't in wolf form, caught her by the elbow before she could hit the ground. Her hands instinctively found purchase against his hard chest.

"Careful there, Healer. I've got you." His voice had a husky timbre, reminding her that she was a female in the presence of a very attractive male.

"I… Thanks."

His eyes glowed amber in the darkness and she could feel his heartbeat, steady and strong, beneath the thin material of his shirt. "You're welcome." He made no move to let her go, and after a few moments she carefully extracted herself from his grip.

The sexual tension she'd been feeling since her arrival had steadily increased, and now it was near suffocating. Gregory and Handell had remained impersonal for her visit, but the rest of the males she'd encountered, including

Simon, *especially* Simon, had exuded a thick vibe of lusty interest.

The Dark Shadow Pack had a low female presence, and the existing males were unable to find willing females in such a remote location. Wolves could mate with humans or Immortals alike, yet it hadn't occurred to her that a single young Witch like herself might be tempting to some of them. Until now.

As soon as she could get a certain big sexy Vampire out of her thoughts, she'd forgo online dating and give Vollmund Hull a call.

A pale grey Wolf yipped and lopped towards them, then seated himself on Keltti's foot, effectively cutting through the sensual tension.

"Thomas?" The Wolf yipped again, his large blue eyes immediately recognizable from the group of males she'd left compound with, before they'd shifted. She hadn't even realized until now that Lycans kept some of the same features in both forms. It made her wonder what color Simon's wolf would be.

"You're so beautiful!" She knelt and ran her fingers through the soft fur, earning a canine sigh of pleasure as the Wolf leaned happily into her hands.

"Thomas!" Ka-Shawn stood between the trees with her hands on her hips in annoyance. "Get away from her!"

The grey Wolf lowered its eyes and slunk away, but Keltti caught the unremorseful smirk he sent her way.

"You can't just pet them like they're a bunch of innocent puppies." Ka-Shawn didn't sound angry, just exasperated. "Would you have groped him like that if he looked like a man?"

Heat bloomed in Keltti's face as she realized she'd breached some sort of Werewolf etiquette rule.

Simon chuckled, giving her a look that said she hadn't screwed up too badly. "We don't get to see a lot of beautiful females at Vollmond Hull; please excuse Thomas' lack of manners." Behind him, Thomas watched her with a grin, his tongue hanging out as he tilted his head sheepishly.

Ka-Shawn saved her from further embarrassment by announcing that they'd reached her favorite destination, and Keltti followed her out of the woods. The little valley held a small lake; the calm water was as black and deep as the sky reflected overhead. Mountains rose behind it, inky black shapes whose outlines could only be seen because of the stars that they blocked out.

"I like to come here to swim. Sometimes I just have to get away from all the political crap at home."

Simon looked surprised and nodded to the lake. "I haven't been here in decades. I forgot it was even here."

Keltti followed the small strip of rocky shore, vaguely aware of the Wolves that dashed back and forth around her, occasionally brushing against her leg as they ran past. A patch of greenery caught her eye, and she ran her fingers through it. It was waist high, and a slightly darker shade of green than the grass around them. Bending to smell them, the scent was not entirely pleasant and somewhat familiar.

"Do you have a knife?" Keltti asked.

Simon produced a slim dagger and held it out to her hilt first.

"Thanks." She used the blade to cut off one of the flower heads that had closed up for the evening. Cutting through it, the soft dark purple petals came apart in her hand.

"Wolfsbane..." Her voice was soft as she thought out loud. Looking back, she realized the Wolves were all giving the patch of weeds a wide berth. "Did you eat any of this?"

Ka-Shawn made a face that showed her horror at the prospect. "No, never!"

Keltti's eyes traveled over the wet soil to the pebbles lining the water. She knelt and scooped up a handful of the liquid and brought it to her nose. The calming scents of fresh earth, grass, dead leaves, and pine were all present, but lurking just beneath the familiar smells was wolfsbane.

"Do you swim here?"

"Yes…" Understanding filled her face as she grasped the implications Keltti was making.

"There's wolfbane in the water." She opened her second sight and Ka-Shawn's aura flared to life. The tiny dark purple lines plaguing her were thicker and more prevalent, making them more noticeable than before. The yellows and pinks were muted, and worried Keltti more than she tried to let on.

She closed her shields, shutting off her second sight as she opened her eyes. The Wolves, no longer frisking back and forth, sat silently with their attention solely on her. Shifters must be more sensitive to the magic she used than she realized.

Slightly uncomfortable with the shine of admiration in their eyes, she stepped out of the wolfsbane patch and turned back the way they came. "I think we've found the source of the problem." She directed her words at Ka-Shawn, but she darted a glance at Simon as she continued. The look he returned was thoughtful with barely concealed reverence.

"No more swimming here. The wolfsbane should eventually leave your system on its own, but I'll give you some herbs to help offset the poison until it's gone. Nightshade, jimson weed, and some mandrake should do the trick. Although… Since you didn't actually ingest any of it, your reaction makes me think you're more sensitive than other Shifters… Kind of like an allergy."

Simon silently traversed the forest ahead of them, stopping to hold back a thick branch. "I had all the wolfsbane exterminated from the property ten years ago; I'll have someone sent out to take care of it immediately."

"How long until I'm back to normal?" Ka-Shawn asked.

"A few weeks, maybe a month. The herbs will help." She didn't know if the female had told her brother how extensively the toxin was affecting her, or if he knew about her inability to shift. "The last of the symptoms to show up, should be the first to go." Ka-Shawn met her eyes uncomprehendingly, and Keltti wiggled her eyebrows suggestively and glanced at the closest Wolf.

"Oh!" The female blushed, obviously not wanting anyone else to know she had temporarily lost the ability to shift.

"I'm surprised no one else has been affected by the wolfsbane. If we hadn't found it now, it would have eventually found its way into our wells." Simon had stopped walking, forcing the females to halt as well.

Keltti nodded, not sure what he was expecting her to say.

"My sister would have continued with her solo adventures and likely poisoned herself to death before we even knew it was happening." Ka-Shawn looked at her shoes, obviously aware that she'd lost the freedom to run alone anymore.

"The Dark Shadow Pack thanks you, Keltti. I am in your debt." She started to tell him it was her pleasure to be able to help a client, but she was startled into silence when Simon knelt before her, bowing his head. The other male Wolves and Ka-Shawn followed suit, dropping gracefully to the ground.

"As Alpha of the Dark Shadow Pack, I acknowledge your service and offer you our friendship."

With his head still bowed, she couldn't see his face to gauge his expression. What was she supposed to say? His words were formal, as if they were part of a ceremony. The silence encroached on her ability to think, and still they waited in their stooped positions.

"Uh... Thank you?"

The Alpha rose smoothly, with everyone else following in a synchronized wave. He reached for her hand and used it to pull her closer into his personal space until their bodies were a scant inch apart. She could smell the masculine musk of sandalwood and spice. His hand was warm, and this time she was prepared for the electric jolt that his contact caused.

"As a friend of the Dark Shadow Pack, you will always be welcome at Vollmund Hull. My Wolves will protect you as one of their own. *I* will protect you, as one of my own."

Whoa—*what?* His look was far too intense for someone who was joking. Behind him, Ka-Shawn was nearly bouncing up and down in excitement. The look the other males gave her made her feel like she was a T-bone steak served up on a silver platter.

Thankfully, the other female put an arm around her and guided her back towards the compound. "Welcome to the Pack, sister."

CHAPTER 11

The hot night settled suffocatingly over Arvid as he crouched next to an old shed. Weeds reeking of summer bloom, taller than his chest, hid his bulky frame as he surveyed the abandoned house. Built in the 1940s, it had been a grand, three-story, southern style building.

Multiple large stone pedestals held square support beams that tapered off at the top, lining the first and second-story wrap around porches. Most of the shutters had succumbed to time and weather and were either missing or being slowly swallowed up by the ground where they had fallen. Small patches of the original paint clung stubbornly to the walls; the bright white now faded to a molted grey. Large chunks of the dark shingles had given way and a few small holes were visible on the roof. The only signs of life were the new sprouts shooting up out of the full eaves.

"On my signal…" Stu's voice came over the comm link, deadly and clear.

Arvid slowed his breathing, cleared everything from his mind but the abandoned acreage. His Vampire senses tingled; someone or something had taken up residence in the house. The air didn't have that sour, rotten feel that he associated with Soul Eaters, but that didn't mean the newest resident was friendly.

He palmed one of his guns and a silver dagger—bullets couldn't always be counted on to do the job. Until he knew what they were up against, he wanted options.

"Three, two, one… *Go!*" Stu's deep voice growled in his

ear, filled with anticipation. The guy had been looking for a fight all week and it was starting to affect the whole team.

Arvid took off at a run. Keeping his back to the house, he cautiously climbed the side stairs. They groaned under his weight and he weaved back and forth around the broken planks.

Tor ghosted up behind him and motioned for him to go first. The door hung open a few inches; a gaping hole stood where the knob should have been. Shame, he always loved a good front kick to breach the door and go in with guns blazing. So dramatic. So Hollywood.

Moving quickly through the stale air, Arvid cleared the west side of the house. No signs of life, just the typical garbage and empties left behind by squatters. Low quality graffiti graced most of the walls, covering several of the ugly, peeling wallpaper styles that had been popular decades ago. It was actually an improvement, in his opinion.

Stu and Ros entered the large, two-story lobby at the same time as Arvid and Tor. Dirt and broken glass crunched under their boots on marble floors that were still mostly intact.

"First floor clear." Stu nodded his acknowledgement and motioned to the stairs. The Warriors fell into formation behind him, and, silently, they ascended the staircase that had once been grand in a different lifetime. The original carpeting had completely degraded to sparse moldy black patches that sent little puffs of dust into the air when they stepped on it.

Arvid turned to check their six o'clock and icy fingers of unease brushed the back of his neck.

Something's off here.

Their original intel had come in the night before that a Soul Eater was possibly squatting here. The King's Army had several civilians on retainer, acting as eyes and ears throughout the city. They were usually fairly reliable.

The second floor was just about cleared when something above them made the faintest of sounds. They froze, everyone scanning the ceiling. Again they heard it; something between a groan of pain and wounded prey caught in a trap.

That was no Soul Eater.

Stu and Ros peeled away from the group and headed for the servant's stairs at the back of the house. Tor followed Arvid up the main stairs, eyes darting in every direction.

Loosing all pretense of stealth, the Warriors flooded the third floor with their presence.

The smells of the lower floors faded, and the sickening perfume of rotting flowers filled Arvid's nose. Something electric caressed his skin; soft and sharp like rose petals and thorns.

It was coming from the large master bedroom; sickly sweet waves of energy that teased at the edges of his awareness. Guns and knives drawn, they prowled further into the room.

"I've got two bodies over here." Rostel's voice came over the comm link.

"Three and a half here." Stu replied.

Three and a half? WTF—

Something pale and ghostly flew out of the shadows, its shriek like breaking metal. It grabbed for Tor, and Arvid squeezed off four rounds; three direct chest hits and one between the eyes. The bullets passed though harmlessly and imbedded themselves in the wall without slowing the creature's attack. Black holes where its eyes should have been turned towards him.

Hello there, ugly.

It was a Witte Wieven. Nasty things; the black widows of the supernatural world. Ghostly females that could glamour men into seeing a beautiful woman. They would lure their prey back to their nest and slowly drain the lifeforce from them, leaving nothing but a mummified husk behind. Occasionally, they were known to eat parts of the body—alive—but that was more for entertainment than for sustenance.

Arvid holstered his gun and pulled a second dagger from his chest harness. She dove at him and he met her halfway with his daggers swinging in a downward arc. She hissed as his hands passed through, leaving two jagged slices in her semi-corporal body. He spun, ready for another round, but Tor beat him by plunging a dagger into her back then slicing another across the space between her head and shoulders. Her cries reached a crescendo with one last wail that ended abruptly. The sudden silence was broken only by a harsh curse from Stu.

The big guy seriously needed a couple hours with a willing female. Or two.

A clean up crew was on their way to erase all signs of the Witte Wieven and her victims. The negative energy left behind would linger for years, deterring humans from the property.

Keltti ignored the growing storm clouds overhead; watching Arvid as he absently ran his fingers over his dagger harness. Underneath he wore a black shirt that said I'M WITH THE DRAGON while a cartoon lizard gave a cocky thumbs-up. He stood stoically contemplating the abandoned house that loomed behind them, uncharacteristically silent. Restless waves of unease rolled off of him.

Kyenel nodded to her from the driver's seat of the black SUV that he'd driven her there in, wordlessly telling her that he'd wait until she was ready. She still wasn't sure why she'd come.

She'd been summoned to Bloddrikker Castle earlier in the day to treat Ranvald for a sword wound that wasn't healing properly. When Kyenel had offered to drive her home, she'd accepted and enjoyed his quirky banter for the ride.

Who knew that not all male Vampires have to be stone-faced and brooding?

An uneasy fluttering in her belly had made her hesitate

at getting out of the vehicle in front of her house. Sometimes the guiding hand of the Goddess wasn't always obvious; and she had learned long ago to trust her Witch's intuition. Kyenel hadn't batted an eye at the unexpected request for a detour.

She hadn't known where to go; they'd just driven east as her awareness had increased. And when they had pulled up next to another of the King's Army's SUVs in the middle of an abandoned acreage, something inside had clicked into place letting her know this was where she was needed.

And she'd managed to shock five huge male Vampires speechless.

Score one for me, she'd thought with a smile.

Confidence had slid into confusion when she realized that none of the Warriors were injured. Still, there had to be a reason she had been pulled here.

Goddess, guide me....

Closing her eyes, she pulled down the shields that protected her empathetic gift and opened her mind to the world around her. Immediately, the strongest emotions nearby flooded her awareness.

Anger and frustration and need pulsed from Stu, reaching for her with a familiarity that spoke of her connection to him. It was a one-way connection, but that wasn't something that she needed to think about now.

Less intense waves of impatience, curiosity, watchfulness and grim satisfaction came from the other Warriors. Just as familiar, because she also had connections with every one of these Vampires. She'd healed each of them; spent time getting to know them. They'd put their lives on the line to keep her safe. They were hers. And that made it so much easier to sift through and find what she was looking for.

There...

The thin line of anxiety coming from Arvid caught her attention. It would have been easy to miss if she wasn't so used to his usual, easy-going arrogance.

She mentally snapped her shields back into place and pulled her shawl snug around her shoulders. The rain was coming; she didn't need her gifts to feel the anticipation in the air.

"What is it?" she asked softly as she approached him.

"I'm not sure..." His voice trailed off as he contemplated the house.

Faking a calm that she didn't feel, Keltti held out her hand towards the pensive Warrior. "May I?"

She was aware of the others watching; waiting to see what would unfold. She liked to think they'd trust her as their healer for more than just their physical ailments. Arvid confirmed her theory by sliding his big hand into hers after only a short moment of hesitation.

Stu's ridged muscles strained to hold him in place as he fought the urge to rip Arvid's arm out of its fucking socket. And then beat him with it. Seeing another male's hand on the Witch wasn't right, and it left him seeing everything through a blistering haze of red.

The wind teased invisible fingers through her silky brunette strands and her long skirt brushed against her calves. Nicely shaped calves that should be wrapped around—

He stopped that thought before it could gain momentum and carry him away.

She wasn't supposed to fucking be here.

She wasn't dressed for being out in the field with his brothers. Her hair was loose around her shoulders instead of tied back, she wore a frilly looking blanket around her shoulders that she'd probably knit herself, and a long skirt with heeled boots. The extra height would have brought her up to his shoulders, if he stood next to her.

"I *feel* it." Her breathless exclamation was filled with wonder. She started towards the house, and immediately her damn impractical boots caused her to lose her footing on the uneven ground. Without even thinking, Stu reached her side and caught her before she could fall. Her grateful smile made his chest tighten with some emotion that he didn't want to identify.

He glowered at Arvid until he released her other hand, while he kept close to her in case she tripped again. He would have kept a hold on her himself, but he could feel the power swirling around her. It might be dangerous to interfere with whatever she was doing; no fucking way did he want to be on the receiving end of that much power if it backlashed.

The house had already been cleared, but Stu followed close behind as they climbed the steps. Becoming complacent in the field could be deadly for a Warrior; and he wasn't going to take any chances with their healer.

Keltti followed the sensation of life. She now knew that's what it was—a tiny sliver of life that beckoned. Arvid felt it too; probably stronger than she did. It was nestled into the fabric of death and pain that comprised the house. She located the stairs that led to the basement and felt around with her foot for the first stair.

"Let me go first." Stu moved past her and disappeared into the shadows. She groped for the wall and found Stu's hand waiting for her instead. His fingers closed over hers, their strength a comfort. Together they descended, and by the time they reached the basement Keltti's eyes had adjusted enough to see the rough outlines of discarded furniture from an earlier era.

"Here." Keltti's hand felt strangely vulnerable as he released it and handed her a flashlight.

"Thanks. You couldn't have let me have it at the top of the stairs?" She thought she caught a flash of his smug grin as he turned away, but she couldn't be sure. It took only a few seconds to orientate herself, and by then Arvid had started ahead of them, seeming to already know where he was going.

"Here." He stopped at a brick-and-mortar wall on the

far side of the basement.

Keltti tapped it with her flashlight; the sound echoing hollowly behind the old bricks. Running her fingers over the wall, she pushed and prodded the bricks hoping to find a loose one.

"There's got to be a way…" she murmured to herself.

She let out a squeak when Stu lifted her out of the way and carried her to the edge of the room before setting her down in a way that was surprisingly gently. He released her slowly, letting her body slide against his until her feet were touching the floor. His hands lingered at her waist; she could feel their warmth through her shirt. Desire reared its ugly head, and her heart skipped a beat.

Stupid sexy Vampires.

"Wait here until we know what we're dealing with." The commanding tone was missing from the order, replaced with an unexpected softness that scared her more than the usual sharp bark he used when they worked together.

"Okay." She wished she had something wittier to say, something to diffuse the suddenly charged air.

She felt his breathing speed up; his hands dug into her a little tighter. His dark eyes staring straight into hers started to glow. Was he going to kiss her? Goddess, she hoped so. She wanted to grab the thick black collar of his coat and pull him down to her lips. Would he taste as good as she remembered? Would he even kiss her back?

He looks like he's ready to devour me. The thought left her breathless, and Stu's eyes glowed brighter as if he could read her mind. Thoughts of his bite surfaced—they were never far—and she knew with certainty that she'd enjoy it; how powerful it would make her feel to slake the hunger of such a strong male.

But that's all she'd be—just a source of blood. Someone to use and toss away. And possibly sex; there was no point in denying the massive erection pressed up against her belly. But that wasn't something she'd settle for. Yes, she wanted him, but she wanted *all* of him.

It seemed unfair that she could ward her mind from just about anything, but there were no wards made to protect her heart.

Stu saw the desire dim from the Witches eyes; felt the slight tensing of her muscles as she prepared to take a step back. And didn't that just feel like a stake in his chest. He turned and stepped away before she could. He heard her stumble as she lost her balance at the sudden loss of support.

Smart girl. She could do better. Deserves better.

His anger came roaring back, wiping out all rational thoughts of why he shouldn't kiss her; quickly replacing them with visions of her delectable body and all the things he wanted to do to it. He growled and spun back towards her, catching her unaware as he backed her in the rough wall and crushed his lips to hers. He slid his tongue against her mouth, demanding she open for him. A very male, very satisfied sigh escaped from him once she granted him access.

Sweet, like honey, he thought. Inhaling deeply, he pulled the scent of her—springtime and fresh things growing—into the very bottom of his lungs.

He wound his hand into her caramel-colored locks, tilting her head back until he could greedily drink from her lips like a drowning man. His other hand skimmed down her back until he could feel the curve of her ass. She moaned into the kiss when he squeezed, and he pulled her even closer so there wasn't a lick of space between them. His leather coat creaked when she pushed it aside to run her hands down his chest. He was momentarily awed by how something so fragile could hold so much power.

Don't be a fucking idiot—you've been wrapped around her finger since you found her. Strange how the thought didn't bother him as much as it should have.

Her hands wandered lower, graceful and demanding at the same time. She unfastened the top button on his leathers with a *pop!* and he froze. Another *pop!* and his cock strained even harder to reach her.

"Keltti, not here…" he protested weakly; sounding to his own ears like a prepubescent youngling. So fucking manly.

They couldn't do this here; not in this shithole where the air stunk of death and fear. She deserved so much better. A soft mattress and silk sheets under her body while he slowly peeled the clothes from her body. Thick drapes on the windows so he could take his time pleasuring her and not even the sun would cut that short. And a hot shower with room for two, once he had thoroughly satisfied her. Wait— no, he couldn't, not without bonding her to him permanently.

One last *pop!* and his cock sprung free, pulling a guttural moan of pure longing from him.

No! Not here… The thought escaped his grasp as her delicate hands seized his manhood; her thumb tracing a path around the sensitive head. She slowly stroked him from root to tip and then back down. He grabbed her by the shoulders, not sure if he intended to push her away or pull her closer. Before he could decide, his whole body tightened, and he tried not to scream like a pansy as an orgasm washed over him; intense waves filling every part of his body as her mere touch brought him more pleasure than he'd ever thought possible.

His traitorous legs threatened to put him on his ass. He framed the Witches slender body with his arms, careful to keep the majority of his weight against the wall for support. His head fell forward to rest on top of hers. The loose wavy strands of her hair tickled his nose, in a nice sort of way, as he struggled to slow his ragged breathing.

Guilt trickled through the fog surrounded him, reminding him of their dank, and possibly dangerous, surroundings. And, of his shamefully short performance.

What the hell had he been thinking? A woman like this shouldn't degrade herself in a place like this. With someone like him. He opened his mouth to apologize but stopped when her slight shoulders started to quiver. Was she crying?

Fucking hell, I made her cry! Stupid son of a bitch—fucking bag of bloody scum—

The Witch tilted her head back and met his eyes with a smile.

She's laughing, he thought with disbelief. *She's fucking laughing.*

"At least we didn't make Arvid wait long." Her eyes danced with mirth and he was suddenly very aware that his dick was still hanging out.

CHAPTER 12

Everybody else had crammed into one of the vehicles's and left. Keltti hadn't felt them leave, her attention having been somewhat occupied by other things. She felt a blush heat her face when Arvid came clomping down the stairs a few minutes later, swinging a large crowbar and making enough noise so she knew he was coming. It was considerate—and obvious that he knew what they'd been doing.

She joined the two Vampires in front of the roughly built wall. It was easier to see now that Arvid had set some high-powered lanterns around the perimeter of the basement. The bricks were a faded red color, stacked floor to ceiling with crumbling grey mortar. Odd, seeing as the rest of the bricks down there were a different shade of red. The mortar also seemed less pitted and worn.

Stu looked between her and Arvid; and finally asked, "You want to do what?"

Arvid shrugged helplessly at her.

"There's something behind the wall. I need to get back there." Yeah, it did sound kinda crazy. The Goddess worked in mysterious ways.

He picked up the crowbar, and muttering something obscene, drove the pointy end into the space between the bricks. Tiny, sharp shards exploded outwards, and the entire wall wavered. A few more well-placed hits and there was a hole big enough to fit a soccer ball through. One kick on either side of the hole by both Warriors and half the wall collapsed. A plume of dust filled the air and made Keltti

111

cough like she had inhaled a ball of dryer lint.

Arvid was already stepping over the pile of rubble, and Keltti hurried to follow. The light inside where her healing gift came from was restless and twitched in her chest. She didn't bother trying to reign in the nervous energy she was sending off; these two hardened Warriors were disciplined enough to ignore a little magical castoff.

"I've got a body!" Arvid called out to them.

Feeling like an idiot, Stu radioed for an evac team to pick up the body.

He'd argued that the clean up crew that was already coming for the Witte Wieven mess could deal with this one too. What was one more fucking body, right?

The Witch had looked horrified, her luminescent green eyes filled with a sheen of tears as she'd stood between him and the body.

"Please Stu! We can't just leave her here!" She'd practically begged, her waves of desperation buffeting him as she held him by the arm. There was a rip on the shoulder of her shirt that caused the front to dip further in the front that it should have, and the pale blue lace cupping her breast peeked out at him. Had she snagged it on the jagged edge of the hole, or had he done that when he'd grabbed her? Smashed mortar dust coated her hair, hiding the glossy honeyed colors. Even covered in grime and cobwebs, she was beautiful.

So, he'd given in and called for an evac.

I will never hear the bloody end of it. His brothers would shit themselves laughing.

Find a dead body? Call the cleaning team. End of story.

Standard procedure in his line of work.

Arvid hadn't said fuck all since they'd found the body. Stu absently realized he must still be in the hidden room. What was so damn important about *this* dead body?

He followed his Witch back into the room to find out.

Keltti stepped past the pile of smashed bricks and held up her flashlight to scan the room.

The body lay in a small bed, neatly tucked into pink bedding greyed with dirt and age. On one side of the room there was a matching dresser with an oval mirror and a small bookshelf holding a variety of fashion magazines, celebrity tabloids, and assorted paperback romance novels. The other side of the room held a large, overstuffed arm chair and a reading lamp. The dirt floor was covered by a pale pink shag carpet. The paintings on the walls appeared to be originals, all in good condition beneath a think layer of dust.

Everything in the room was in remarkably good condition; even the body. It was a female, her long red hair spilling out over the pillowcase onto the sheets. There were dancing rabbits and rainbows on her nightgown, the neckline rimmed with pink satin and a bow. Her skin was dry like parchment paper, pulled tight around her bones.

Arvid stood near the foot of the bed staring down at her, his face unreadable.

Please Goddess, guide me…

Kneeling by the bed, Keltti softly touched the female's arm and opened herself up to her second sight. Immediately her peripheral was blinded by the Warriors' auras; both a pulsing red that blazed with strength and health. Like the two males, they were slightly different from each other but totally familiar to her.

She forced her attention away them and gently probed the room for a sign as to why she had been led here. There had to be a reason; there must be *something* that she was supposed to do here. Allowing her mind to wander, she skimmed through the house, skirting the bodies on the third floor, finding nothing out of place. Widening her search, the soft glow of some field mice and a rabbit darted across her awareness. Their little hearts raced as they held perfectly still in their homes, sensing the large predators that had invaded their territory.

Don't worry guys; the big bad Vampires won't hurt you.

She couldn't send them any healing waves of reassurance without getting closer, but animals could usually pick up on her feelings and were surprisingly empathetic themselves. Taking a deep breath, she slowly let it out and felt her body undo the tension that had chased away her tranquility. She tuned out the leftover emotions swirling through the air: fear, fury, and desperation that didn't belong to her. Calm settled over her like warm bath water, and even the Vampire's swirling auras slowed.

But she still had the nagging feeling that she was missing something. What was she not seeing?

Let's try something different…

A healer is made of two things: raw talent and the training to use that talent. Keltti had an abundance of both. Her mind scanned back over her years of training in Iceland; hundreds of hours of classes, studying, hands-on practical application and practice, all guided by the very best and brightest of her craft. Now, one particular lesson stood out.

"Your own emotions can help add to your power, but they can also be your biggest hindrance. Embrace your feelings; use their power." Nothing like a cryptic tid-bit of information stored in the back of your brain to get things moving.

Well here goes nothing…

Holding out her free hand, she reached towards the Vampire who had been a daily constant in her mind for the last five years. There was a mountain of emotions that she'd come to associate with him; some good, some not so good, but all of them strong. If there was even a chance that she could harness some of that power, she would.

"Give me your hand." He offered it without hesitation or protest, sliding his rough scarred palm into hers.

She took the proffered energy, siphoning it into her second sight. And then she saw it: a tiny spark in the dark, dim room, almost unnoticeable next to the bright Vampire auras. It called to her like a lighthouse cutting through a gale; weak and frail but undeniable to her senses, nonetheless.

"She's alive!" Keltti whispered in satisfaction.

What a fucked-up night.

The Captain ended up summoning the Witch to the castle a few times per week, whenever a soldier came back injured beyond what a blood donation and some shut eye could fix. Their ranks were down, and every Warrior was needed in top shape at all times. Keltti no longer came out on patrol with them, and thank the Gods for that. She didn't belong in the death filled trenches of a war that wasn't even hers. But she still dropped whatever she was doing when someone was down in the field. And she lived a hell of a lot closer than Bloddrikker Castle—practically downtown.

She wasn't supposed to be here tonight. Goosebumps rose on his arms; something was going on here and Stu didn't like it one fucking bit.

Stu watched the evac team, Adrian and Ros, as they gently loaded the woman's body onto a stretcher. Apparently, she was still alive. He didn't see how that was possible; his Vampire senses couldn't hear a heart beat or any breathing.

There was some discussion about what to do with her; Keltti wanted her brought back to the Healing Grove, but Arvid thought the castle infirmary was best. The argument receded into background noise as Stu leaned against the wall and surveyed the basement.

He was tired.

So fucking tired.

The war was taking its toll on him. The Rebels had been uncharacteristically quiet for a while now; something big was coming. And they were busy chasing the influx of other predators that had moved into the city; too busy to properly investigate what the Sterken bastards were up to. Not enough good males to go around; Calgary was a hell of a metropolis. They should be doing more recruiting. Vampires were long-lived and hard to kill, but their numbers still dwindled. Adding to their ranks wasn't as easy as the movies made it look; Vamps were born, not made. The world would be overrun if it were as easy as draining a human dry and then force feeding the body some Vamp blood.

His lip curled in distain; fucking Hollywood and their bizarre notions of his kind. Fucking bad hair and sparkling diamond skin shit. WTF were they thinking?

CHAPTER 13

The heat of the day had given way to a humid evening. This Indian summer was hanging on for longer than Keltti had dared hope for. A light breeze hinted at a coming storm; and she wondered if she were the only one who could taste the expectation in the air. An involuntary shiver... Something was coming.

"Keltti! Over here!" Ka-Shawn's voice carried over the heads of the bar crowd on the busy sidewalk, her arms waving overhead.

She looks a million times better, Keltti thought with satisfaction.

It had only been a week since she'd given Ka-Shawn some herbs to counteract the wolfsbane, but the difference was noticeable. She glowed with health and happiness; partially due to her supernatural genes but most of it came from the vibrant essence that made her the woman she was. That much spirit was hard to dim, even from human eyes.

Tonight, she was sheathed in a slinky red dress that artfully hung off one shoulder, leaving the other bare and calling attention to the long, graceful column of her neck. It clung to just the right spots, leaving room for her to move comfortably. She didn't wear a bra and there were no underwear-lines, Keltti noticed with envy.

Her newfound confidence finally matched her status as a vibrant immortal in the prime of her life. Werewolves were far less inhibited than humans; Witches hovered somewhere between the two, but Keltti had always leaned closer to modesty than others of her kind and found herself envious of the female Shifter.

Ka-Shawn waited for her with six other Werewolves—all of them male—including Simon. They smoothly parted ranks to make room for her, sheltering her from the current of the bodies moving around them.

"Healer, it's a pleasure to see you again." Simon's voice caressed her, lingering like a hot muggy night under open skies; his hand taking hers. He wasn't really shaking it—just holding it between them while his thumb stroked over her pulse. Which started to pound a little faster.

Whoa, down girl. Just breathe.

He was impeccably dressed in an emerald green polo shirt and distressed jeans, his dark hair freshly cut in a popular style that made him look scholarly, yet trendy.

"Hi." Her voice sounded a little shaky, even to her own ears, as introductions were made and pleasantries were exchanged. She was finally able to extract her hand when Ka-Shawn announced, "Let's go! I want to *dance!*" and dragged her by the arm towards the bar.

The Siren's Call was located in the heart of downtown Calgary and welcomed all supernaturals. Keltti spotted a few humans and wondered if they knew they weren't at the top of the food chain in here. Probably, since they wouldn't have gotten by the bouncer without an escort.

The bass was loud, seeping into one's bones and cocooning everything in a solid wall of sound so that conversation was next to impossible. The Werewolves had come prepared with small earplugs to protect their sensitive hearing.

Ka-Shawn had introduced Keltti to certain drinks, a whole new world of wonderful, between songs. The one she currently held was called "Sex with Jennifer" and was a magical combo of tropical sultry goodness. One of the Wolves—Thomas? —took the empty glass from her hand. When had she finished that one?

Simon slid his arm around her waist and guided her to

the dancefloor; the pulsing beat made her head spin, and she was glad she had a someone to hold onto. His solid strength was reassuring. Her body, leaning into his like gravity, was no longer governed by the laws of physics. He let her lead, his hips following the movement of hers gracefully, leaving a bare inch between their bodies. It was a surprisingly gentlemanly thing to do; the place was full of writhing bodies grinding and pressing into each other.

Simon smiled down at her and she found herself laughing aloud with the pure joy of giving her body over to the music. He was definitely exuding sexual undertones towards her, but she had simply ignored them so far. He didn't press her or try anything inappropriate and she was grateful to leave it at that. She wasn't ready to take that step yet.

She'd been surprised when Ka-Shawn had called and invited her out. Apparently, the Dark Shadow Pack wasn't entirely against socializing with others. It made sense that they'd want to get out once in a while and blow off some steam. She thought the males' primary goal would have been finding willing females, but they hadn't left their Alpha's presence, aside from getting more drinks.

Her cell was tucked into her back pocket, but she'd turned it off. The King's Warriors would have to fend for themselves—she was taking the night off.

But what if they need me?

The thought of Stu taking a bullet... Her steps faltered and Simon pulled her closer to steady her.

"What is it?" His voice was full of genuine concern and Keltti felt like a schmuck. This was the closest she'd come to having real friends in a long time and she was ruining it. Firmly pushing all thoughts of big sexy Vampires into the very back of her mind, she looked up at Simon with what she hoped was a reassuring smile.

"Nothing, just too much to drink."

"I'm glad you came out tonight. I'm very grateful for your help with Ka-Shawn." His words were like liquid silk, sliding around her body intimately. How did he do that?

A slower song started, the lights dimming even further. The floor cleared a bit, as party-goers left to acquire more beverages.

"Care to dance, little Witch?" Keltti turned to find a Vampire standing with his hand out in invitation. Blond hair artfully teased into a careless wave brushed the collar of the white dress shirt that he wore in a charmingly casual way, with the top three buttons undone. His eyes were a flat brown and held just the right amount of hope and eagerness to make him seem innocent.

Simon pulled her against his body as three of his Wolves melted out of the shadows directly in front of the Vamp. "Sorry mate, her card's already full." The Alpha tone in his voice was unmistakable and left no room for discussion.

The Vamp raised his hands in surrender and backed away into the sea of couples dancing.

"Let's dance." He deftly pulled her into the rhythm of the slow dance before she could protest. Her irritation rose, hot and sharp, and she tried to swallow it down. It wasn't Simons fault—his macho attitude just reminded her of a certain Vampire that she was trying to forget about.

After the earth-shattering kiss she'd shared with Stu, she'd expected… Something. *Anything.* But nothing had changed. Whatever walls he was hiding behind were as tall as ever. Well, screw him and his walls. Tonight was just for her.

Stu tracked a Soul Eater down a damp alley, ripe with the smell of wet garbage and stale beer. Muffled bass from a number of bars in the area collided with the excited chatter of voices as people milled about on the sidewalk.

The Soul Eater must've just jumped on the soul sucking wagon, because he looked lucid; only the ripe smell of rotting flesh gave him away. Wearing a light purple dress shirt and khakis, he turned out of the alley and headed towards the Siren's Call. Not the usual hunting ground for a Soul Eater; any humans there would already be spoken for. It was possible he was meeting someone. Or maybe he just wanted to knock back a few cold ones. Either way, he was as good as fucking dead.

Waiting until his target had gone inside; Stu disengaged from the shadows and followed. The bouncer wisely kept his mouth shut. The King's Army was well known, affording him an unspoken measure of respect from other supernaturals. The pulsing noise washed over him; a thick cocktail of alcohol and the pheromones of various species looking to mate assaulted his nose.

What the fuck…

A tingling awareness slid through his body, followed closely by disbelief and then red-hot fury. She was here. *His* Witch.

His body was responding to her nearness before his brain even knew what the hell was happening. Catching a hint of her fresh earthy scent, he scanned the room and zeroed in on the dance floor. He still couldn't see her; she was shorter than most of the females who were here in their four-inch teetering heels.

"I've got a situation; send backup. Siren's Call on 9th."

"On our way," his comm line cracked back.

The Soul Eater was already forgotten. Stu's body vibrated like a tuning fork as he tracked his new prey. The enthusiastic, gyrating dancers parted as he made his way towards a particularly loud group of males dancing.

Werewolves. Typical. And there in the middle of group was Keltti.

Aqua colored jewels held her soft honey locks away from her face; she'd curled it tonight and it bounced around her shoulders as she danced. A wispy scarf in the same aqua color was tied around her neck. Her tank top, white lace over white fabric, offered a sweet hint of the cleavage that hid beneath. And the short jean skirt was longer than anything the other females were wearing, but still displayed the curve of her legs, from mid-thigh all the way down to the tiny sandal straps that criss-crossed her ankles and toes. He took it all in, every beautiful inch, and clenched his fists in an effort to remind himself that she wasn't his. Besides, murdering a Pack of Wolves would be highly frowned upon by his superiors.

The thought that she had chosen to be there tonight, to be with another male, made him sick. He wanted to throttle the bastard. And then put a few rounds in his heart. And maybe throttle him some more. Right after he cut the guy's dick off.

Stu watched as another woman in a red dress leaned into her and said something that made them both laugh; the sight hitting him like a punch to his solar plexus and taking his breath away. Damn.

A male next to her caught her by the hand and spun her around twice and into the waiting hands of another. Stu was moving before she'd even come to a complete stop, slamming into the second male and sending him flying away from her. Keltti came to a halt against Stu's chest and he wrapped an arm around her possessively as the male came at them.

"*Stu?* What—" He pulled her behind the bulk of his body as the bastard—a Wolf, Stu noted—struck him in the jaw. His fangs cut into his lip and he spit out a mouthful of blood.

"Get away from her!" The weight of the words settled over Stu, trying to force obedience. So, the Wolf was an Alpha. How nice for him. Too bad that mojo shit didn't work on him.

More Wolves clustered around their Alpha, drawn in by the fight and smell of freshly spilt blood. If they'd so much as hurt one hair on his Witch's beautiful head, he was going to tear them apart.

"Let go of me!" Keltti kicked him in the back of his calf, and he let go of her out of concern that she'd keep kicking him and injure her bare toes. She got right in his face, ineffectually pushing against his chest to separate him from the Pack that had dared touch what was his.

"Back *off!* What is *wrong* with you!?!" The heat from her hands seeped into him, helping calm his body's demand for violence. He leaned down and let her scent wash over him. She was all right. They hadn't hurt her. He didn't have to murder anyone—she'd probably be angry at him if he did.

"You know this clown?" The Alpha's casual voice was directed at Keltti, but his eyes never left Stu.

"Yes, he's…" He could read the unspoken words in her clear green eyes as if she was whispering them in his head. *He used me. He pushed me away. He hurt me.* Stu could read every thought as it crossed her mind and even felt some of the pain. Or maybe that was just his. Knowing what he'd done to her was like a fucking knife in his chest. Gods, he was going to spend the rest of his life making it up to her.

"…Nobody. He's nobody." The words hung in the air between them for what felt like forever. He forgot about the Wolves and the hundreds of bodies surrounding them; forgot how to fucking breath. There was resignation and disappointment and pity in her expression. It was like a hundred sucker punches to the gut, doubling him over and letting her slip through his fingers.

He felt, rather than saw, Ros, Kye and Tor ghost up behind him.

"Problem, Stu?" Kye drawled, intentionally casual to break the mounting tension.

Yeah, big fucking problem here.

He was nobody. An absolute *nobody* to her. He could've lived with being an asshole. As long as he was *her* asshole. But a nobody? That was harsh. But entirely deserved since he'd done nothing but push her away.

The Alpha was still standing stoically with his arms crossed, his Wolves flanking him, their bodies tense and eager for a fight. Perfect. With the way tonight way going, Stu could use a good old-fashion hand-to-hand throwdown.

For goodness sakes, what is wrong with all these over-possessive, territorial, testosterone-filled idiots? They were acting like a bunch of Neanderthals. Swinging their clubs and pounding their chests; Keltti was surprised they hadn't started dragging random females out by their hair. Or peeing on the walls to mark their territory.

"There's no problem, we were just about—" She tripped on something—possibly her own foot—and went careening into Tor's huge chest. "Ouch, sorry Tor." The silent Warrior steadied her with one hand, keeping his dagger hand free, she noticed, while she struggled to find her balance.

Suddenly Stu was there, grabbing her by the arms and pulling her against his firm body. The look he gave Tor was anything but friendly.

"Let go! You are such... Such a *caveman!*" Even Stu looked a little surprised at her accusation. His dark eyes studied her, letting her feel the weight of his gaze as it skimmed over every inch of her. She shivered, unable to deny that she still wanted him. His pupils dilated and he leaned in until his face was touching hers, his breath hot on her neck as he took in her scent.

"Are you... *drunk?*" Wait... What was he asking? No, of course she wasn't.

"Noooooo..." *Oh man, maybe I do sound drunk*, she thought sheepishly.

Tor smirked and she shot him a dirty look.

"That's it, we're leaving." Stu's declaration caused Simon to take a step forward, and Keltti could see their auras collide with each other. It was beautiful and violent and blinding; and she struggled to shut out her second sight. The kaleidoscope of colors and energies was making her dizzy. Maybe she really was drunk.

"You can't tell me what to do! It's my night off."

"The hell I can't." He started to drag her across the room towards the doors, her sandals offering no traction on the hardwood. The Wolves had them surrounded before they'd gone no more than half a dozen steps. Knives came out. Apparently, even Wolves carried them.

I really should get my own. All the cool kids were doing it.

Six Wolves against four Vamps; they were pretty evenly matched. Some of the dancers were starting to catch on that something big was about to happen. A hush fell over the crowd, even though the music continued to blare.

"She's with me tonight, mate." Simon sounded every bit the entitled leader he was, right down to the haughty slant of his dark eyebrows.

"She's with *me* tonight. And tomorrow. And the night after that. She's with me *every* fucking night from now on. She's *mine.*" Stu's arm tightened around her, his words sending a jolt of pleasure through her until she gave herself a mental slap to snap out of this dangerous delusion.

"What are you talking about?" *You don't want me. You don't want anything to do with me.* Was this some sick twisted game of his to stomp a little harder on her heart?

"She's my… My life-mate." He actually sounded genuine. She resisted the urge to laugh; that would just be childish and cruel. If he was telling the truth. Which he probably wasn't. But, even the Wolves looked a little stunned. Behind them, Ka-Shawn chortled. Keltti wished she could turn around to see Stu's face, but there was no give in his grip.

"I don't see a mark," Simon remarked thoughtfully.

"Maybe it's under her clothes," one of the Wolves commented.

"Maybe he hasn't marked her at all," another Wolf added helpfully.

"Maybe it's none of your darn business! And maybe you should stop talking about me like I'm not standing right here!" Keltti snapped.

This was absolutely ridiculous. She drove her elbow into the rock-hard abs behind her, earning herself a good-sized bruise in the process, but was rewarded by Stu letting her go. The Vampires parted ranks to allow her through and she headed for the exit. She'd had her fill of fun tonight and was ready to go home.

Stu waited until she was outside before wrapping an arm around her shoulders and guiding her into the nearest alley, despite her protests. Now that the adrenaline was fading from his system, he could think more clearly.

"What the hell do you think you were doing in there?" He kept his voice calm, betraying none of the fear, jealousy or rage he'd felt at finding her in the midst of a near-orgy with a Pack of mutts.

"Sex in the jungle." She smiled fondly, as if trying to recall more. "And Sex on the Beach. Those were my favorite; *sooo* good."

He had her pinned against the rough brick wall before he'd even realized he was moving; his vision turned an angry shade of red and he knew his eyes were glowing. Fury flowed like hot lava through his veins, scorching away all thought and reason. "You did *what*—" He couldn't finish, his words getting stuck as his fangs descended.

She laughed, a girlish little sound that wrapped itself around his cock, inviting it to join in the conversation. The urge to complete the bonding was primal, demanding he claim what was rightfully his. She had no idea the danger she was courting. No idea how close he was to taking her right then and there in this alley. He wanted the Wolves to see his bite on her pale neck, smell his scent all over her body and most of all, he wanted the whole fucking world to see his mating mark on her skin.

"And the one that was blue—I don't remember what it was called... It was sweet like a peach. Oh! Sex in the driveway. That one was tasty too."

"What the hell are you talking about?" His ire receded a little to make room for a whopping dose of confusion.

"The drinks; they were good. I liked them; much better than wine."

Gods above, she *was* drunk. Feeling like a jerk, he let the anger wash out of him along with the tension that had been holding him tighter than a bow string. It wasn't her fault; what kind of male would he be if he satisfied his primal urges on her when she was obviously intoxicated? The lowest kind of male.

"Let's get you home, Sunshine." It came out gruffer than he intended so he softened his words with a kiss on her forehead.

"Stu?"

He hadn't said anything during their walk to the SUV that was parked a few blocks away. Her head didn't feel like it was full of quilt-batting anymore and the silence had given her time to think. "Did you mean what you said back there?"

He started the vehicle and pulled out into traffic before he answered. "Yeah, every word of it."

"Why didn't you say anything before?"

"The potential to make you my mate is there, but it doesn't mean we have to... Ah, *do anything* about it."

"Oh." She tried to keep the hurt and disappointment out of her voice. Of course, he'd want to avoid any permanent bond to her. His earlier words at the club had stirred up a well of hope inside her that she'd been stupid enough to latch onto.

Stop being so needy, she mentally chastised herself.

"So, the other night at the abandoned farmhouse, that didn't count?" She couldn't help the blush that heated her face.

"I didn't bite you. And technically speaking, we didn't actually... You know, do anything that would count."

She'd learned a good bit about other supernaturals and their mating habits while she'd been in Iceland; but now she was questioning the accuracy of the info. A mating bond was supposed to be something rare and wonderful; yet Stu was acting like it was a death sentence. But maybe to him, being bonded with her *was* a death sentence.

Tears stung her eyes and she tried to blink them away. *Don't cry now. You're almost home, just a few more minutes and you can break down there.*

"Why did you even mention it? It's been five years." Plenty of time for her to stop thinking about him. In theory.

Pulling to a stop in front of her little bungalow, he shut the engine off and turned towards her. He grabbed her hand before she could bail, waiting until she would look him in the eye. "Five years, I've waited for this to stop; this need, Gods, I can't get you out of my head. Five years, Keltti!" He was yelling now, his eyes glowing with some emotion she couldn't name. "Five *years*, trying to do the right thing! Five years of going to sleep every night with *this*—" He cupped the front of himself, and she gasped at the sight of the huge erection tenting his leathers. "—But now I'm done! You. Are. *Mine.*"

He pulled her down, crushing her lips against his in a bruising kiss. Her mouth opened of its own volition, inviting him to explore every inch. He breathed greedy little sounds into her as he plundered, demanding she give him everything she had.

The familiar desire that filled her every time she was around this male flooded her, making her back arch and a moan escaped her lips. He dragged her over the center console and into his lap so that she was straddling him, never breaking their kiss. She shifted, trying to get closer to alleviate the ache he'd created.

"Keltti— "

She tugged at her skirt but the damn thing clung to her thighs like wet saran-wrap.

"—*Sunshine*—" His voice was ragged and cut though her haze of desire. "Please, we have to stop."

"What?" Goddess, she was so confused. Did he want her or not?

They were both breathing hard, and he was visibly torn between letting her go and continuing to ravish her.

"I've had a long time to think about this." His leather coat protested as his chest expanded and contracted on a sigh. "It took five years for my head to figure out what my body knew all along: you're *mine*. You've been mine since the night I met you. I can't fight this anymore. This whole bonding thing is just too fucking strong…"

"Do you *want* to fight it?"

"I did. I tried to. But now… I can't do it anymore. Gods, I feel… I have no fucking idea what I'm doing." His words were blunt, but she could sense the vulnerability beneath them. It wouldn't be easy for such a proud, strong male to admit what he just did.

"If you don't want this, tell me now. Nothing has to change; I'll still protect you with my life in the field. I won't force this on you." His eyes were sincere, like he truly believed she might not want him.

The big dummy still had no idea. None. It was well past time she educated him.

CHAPTER 14

Stu kicked the door of the SUV open, still holding his Witch—*his mate*—in his arms. Gods, he needed to get her inside. Before she changed her mind about him. Before she realized she could do a hell of a lot better.

His powerful stride ate up the distance to the house and he set her down to unlock the door. She stepped inside and looked back over her shoulder to see if he was still with her. *Every damn night, Sunshine, I'll be here every damn night.* Her smile was open and honest, and she made no effort to hide the excitement and anticipation that she felt.

He felt it as soon as his boot crossed the threshold of the door and touched the floor: another Vampire. Close. Too close to call for backup. His guns hadn't even cleared his holsters when a bullet tore into his shoulder. It went straight through, the force of the impact spinning him sideways against the doorframe. His right arm hung uselessly, refusing to grasp the gun.

Keltti screamed and reached for him. Someone grabbed her from behind, lifting her off her feet with one arm around her neck, the other around her waist, still holding the gun they'd used to shoot him.

"Back off soldier, this one is ours." Spit flew from his lips, his eyes darting side to side, as he searched for a way out now that Stu blocked the front door.

Adrenaline pounded through Stu's body, his instincts shouting at him to protect her. He leveled his gun at the motherfucker with his good arm, but he couldn't bring himself to pull the trigger. Not with it pointed so close to his mate. The bastard was going to pay for threatening his Witch.

"Let her go." He let his training take over, keeping his voice cool, using his heightened senses to scan the rest of the house for any other threats.

A second bullet ripped into him, this time in his lower back. The pain was blinding and knocked him to his knees; his vision went black for a few precious seconds. He could hear his Witch struggling with her captor, and that was enough to bring him back from the edge of passing out. Something in the kitchen smashed and he felt pride for his stubborn, independent mate swell in his chest. He should have known she wouldn't go willingly.

Get your head in the game, Warrior!

Struggling to his feet, he realized his second gun was gone, dropped when he'd been shot. He palmed a dagger and surged further into the house, away from the direction the second bullet had come from. The male that had his mate would be the first to bleed, and then he'd take care of whoever had snippered him from the front yard.

The kitchen was dark, lit only by the moonlight shining through the window above the sink. Two potted plants on the counter were knocked over, and a third lay smashed on the floor. Dirt and broken bits of pottery clung to the crazed Vamps hair and shoulders. His Witch was turning out to be a feisty little hellfire.

Her attacker let go of her neck to wipe the dirt out of his eyes, and she used the opportunity to turn in his remaining arm so that she was facing him. He fumbled blindly to hold onto her; but she wasn't trying to pull away from him, instead, she wiggled her arms up and leaned her whole body into his. Gently, she placed her palms on either side of his face. He must have sensed that she'd turned the tables on him somehow, and he started to back away from her. Fear made him clumsy; he banged his hip into the corner of the cupboard and then smacked his head on the cupboards above. His pale skin started to glow, and he screamed as light started to pour from his open mouth. Stu stumbled forward, trying to get to her, ready to put his body between her and whatever new threat the Vamp posed. Before he could reach them, the shrieking male's head exploded with a small *bang!* sending out a shower of black goo. The rest of his body slumped heavily to its knees and tipped onto its side between Stu and his mate. More black goo oozed sluggishly from its gaping neck.

What the fuck?

He didn't have time to ponder whatever the hell had just happened; he could see Keltti's hands starting to shake and feel the distress filling her. He stepped over the body, stopping long enough to twist one of his daggers in its heart—you never could be too cautious with those sly bastards—and pulled his mate into his arms.

"What did I *do*?" Her words were muffled against his chest, and he was pretty sure she was crying. His shirt was warm and wet, but that could have been from his blood. Or the black goo that she was covered in. What the hell was that shit?

He didn't have an answer for her, so he just murmured what he hoped were soothing sounds into her hair as he held her. Gods, he had no idea what he was doing. None. He should be out killing something, anything, doing his job as her mate to protect her. There should be a fucking manual about the whole mating bond. Still, he must be doing something right, because she wasn't shaking as violently anymore. He held her tighter, her body fitting perfectly against his.

"Stu? Look at me." She sounded far away; when had she left?

He opened his eyes to find her exactly where he'd left her. Her eyes were a radiant green, all the more vibrant because of the darkness around them.

"Stu, what's wrong?" Her worry penetrated the calm that had settled over his body. He felt cold, his arms and legs too heavy to lift. The burning pain in his shoulder and back that he had pushed to the back of his mind during the fight came roaring back with a vengeance, and he bit back a cry.

"We shhh… should go." His tongue felt thick and slurred the simple words.

"Oh no! You're shot!" He heard her pull up his shirt. He must've shut his eyes again, because he couldn't see anything.

"Twice." Gods, he felt weak.

"*Twice?!?* Why didn't you say anything?" She was searching with her healing powers; he could feel the warmth sliding under his skin and through his body. "We need to get you back to the infirmary."

She dragged him through the house and back out the front door. The fresh air helped some of his alertness return.

And then someone shot him. Again.

Something was wrong.

Hadley shivered, and it had nothing to do with the temperature in the room. The weird broken part of her brain that had been leading her north for the last two months suddenly lit up like a Christmas tree. She got to her feet, her quick movements barely registering with the two strung-out junkies on the other side of the room.

Unease bloomed in her gut, and she quickly shouldered her beat up backpack. There was nothing to pack. She kept everything ready to go at a moment's notice. She took the quickest way out, climbing through the bedroom window and dropping lightly to her feet in the backyard. It was just as abandoned and strewn with garbage as the house had been. At least out here, the smell could dissipate a little.

She felt marginally better that she was no longer trapped by four walls, but the prickly ache in her stomach told her she wasn't out of danger yet. She'd learned long ago to trust her gut, so she let her body lead her down the alley. A painful pounding started in her head and she knew what lay ahead. Monsters. Her headaches always came when monsters were close by. The pounding intensified, and she knew they were getting closer.

Usually, she could feel their attention seeking her and sometimes zeroing in on her, stalking her. But, tonight was different; the slimy fingers of awareness weren't probing the dark and searching for her. They must be hunting something else. A pang of pity for their victim was quickly brushed aside; useless thoughts like that would make her sloppy and get her killed.

Her unease ratcheted up into near panic, trying to tell her she wasn't going to make it in time.

In time for what?

The distinct *pop!* of a gunshot sounded about a block away, in the same direction she was being pulled. She'd always been led away from the monsters, had always managed to stay one step ahead of their relentless pursuit by trusting her instincts. And now that she was being led directly to them, she hesitated for only a heartbeat before breaking into a run.

Keltti went down under the weight of Stu's hard body. He used their momentum to roll towards the old oak in her front yard, and she helped drag him the rest of the way until they had the tree at their backs.

"Are you okay?" His voice was strained as he scanned the area.

"Me? You just got shot! *Again!*"

A bullet bit into the tree, sending tiny pieces of bark flying. Stu pushed her further into the shelter of the oak; the shooter must be in one of the yards across the street. Pulling out his backup piece, he held it steadily in his good hand. He growled something into his comm link, hopefully calling for backup.

"The keys are still in the SUV. I'll cover you. Don't wait for me, just get the hell out of here."

"No!" Horror filled her at the thought of leaving him behind.

"On my count."

"Stu, no! I can heal you."

"There's no time. I won't make it that far." He peered around the tree and squeezed off a couple of shots.

"Three...two..." She couldn't leave him. There had to be another way.

Goddess, please—

Squealing tires and the sudden shriek of metal on metal interrupted any further arguments about leaving without him. A grey sedan slid to a stop in the middle of Keltti's lawn, throwing up clumps of grass and dirt, and leaving two small ruts across the otherwise well-kept property. A small blonde woman jumped out of the driver's seat and opened the back door.

"Get in!" She looked at them expectantly, hunching even lower when another round of bullets flew over her head. "Come on!" Nearly bent in half, she looked terrified and nothing like the backup Keltti was expecting. But they couldn't stay here forever; Stu must be getting low on ammunition, and she could sense his strength fading.

"Let's *go!*"

"Keltti, no! We have no idea who she's working for! Backup's on the way—"

"Not soon enough! Move it! *Now!*"

Shoving her shoulder under the bulk of his weight, Keltti did her best to help drag the stubborn male to the waiting car. His shoulder had already partially healed, but the last bullet must have hit him in the leg, because it wouldn't support any of his weight on it.

They made it the short distance to the car, and she scooted across the back seat before Stu hauled himself in. The car peeled out of her yard before they had even shut the door.

"Who are—" Stu's unconscious body landed in Keltti's lap as they rounded a particularly sharp corner.

"Oh, hi. I'm Hadley." The small woman in the driver's seat smiled back at them.

Keltti had poured every ounce of healing light she had into Stu's damaged body. The second bullet had lodged itself in his hip bone, and it clung stubbornly as she wrestled to free it. By the time she had removed it, the poison had spread throughout his body. His breathing was shallow, and she could feel his heart stuttering.

The gates of Bloddrikker Castle had swung open, and immediately Kye and Vernar surrounded the car with their weapons drawn.

Keltti banged on the window to get their attention. "It's me! Stu's injured, get out of the way!" Vernar said something into his comm link and lowered his gun.

Hadley had wisely kept her mouth shut and shuffled over into the passenger seat when Kye motioned with his gun. He climbed in and threw the car into drive, speeding into the underground parkade. More Warriors were waiting with a stretcher, and they carefully lifted Stu out of the car.

Keltti ignored their barrage of questions, focusing on pouring all her energy into Stu's broken body, trying to break down the toxin that was killing him. She gripped his hand tightly, refusing to let go even when they reached the infirmary.

Goddess, please help him!

Eventually, the room grew quiet, everyone else having left. She could have opened her eyes to check but really didn't care. That would have taken effort, and right now all her effort was focused on one very important male. Her body grew shaky and cold, but still, she continued to fight the poison. One by one, everything faded from her awareness until all she knew was the feel of his hand in hers.

Then, nothing.

Stu woke slowly. That alone was worrisome; he was always conscious of his surroundings. Trying to remember where he was felt like running through mud that was three feet deep. With bricks in his boots. And a semi-truck strapped to his back.

The first thing that caught his attention were the fingers intertwined with his. His little Witch. He'd know her soft touch anywhere. He caught her familiar scent and inhaled deeply to capture more of it.

Cracking his eyes open, he was greeted with the familiar sight of her head pillowed on his arm. Her hair tickled his chest through the tears in his shirt. He could see his healed bullet wound peeking out, red and angry, but no longer open or bleeding. His back hurt like a son of a bitch. His leg wound must've healed, at least partially, because he could move both of his feet again.

Overall, his body felt like shit-on-a-stick, but a streak of happiness shot through him at the sight of the female sleeping next to him. A male could get used to this.

The door opened on smooth hinges and Vernar and Arvid strode in. Keltti stirred and sat up, stretching her back as far as the stiff chair would allow. Her face, still covered in black goo and dried blood, lit up when she saw he was awake.

"Stu!" Her joy was like a balm over his entire body, washing away some of the lingering pain.

"Stu, glad to see you're awake." He tore his eyes away from his Witch, to look at his commanding officer.

"What the hell happened?"

And wasn't that the fucking million-dollar question. What the hell, indeed.

Kye sat at the metal interrogation table, watching the small blonde woman across from him. Hadley, she said her name was. No last name; just "Hadley."

Her old backpack had been thoroughly searched and returned to her; she now sat hunched in the uncomfortable chair clinging to it.

"Why are you here, Hadley?" He kept his voice neutral, bordering on friendly.

"I don't know."

"How did you find the injured soldier and our healer?"

"I don't know. I just saw they were in trouble. Something was shooting at them."

"Someone or some*thing*?" Her eyes momentarily revealed her dismay at the slipup.

So, she knew that humans weren't the only ones out there. Interesting.

What else does she know? Most humans were totally ignorant to the supernatural world, yet this one had stepped in to help his brother-in-arms. Very, very interesting.

"How did you find Bloddrikker Castle?"

"Is that where we are? It wasn't hard—it's all lit up. You can see the glow from downtown." The multiple layers of glamour should have made it invisible to all human eyes. Jeez, even he couldn't see it from the city.

She squirmed in her seat, continuing to cast glances between Kye, the large mirror, and the door; she obviously wanted to leave. But Kye wasn't ready to let her go yet; not until the possibility of a threat had been eliminated completely.

"Who's Bert Dunworth?" He switched topics, watching for any sign of recognition in her face. Her eyebrows rose even higher, and confusion made her violet eyes even paler than before.

"Who?"

"He owns the car that you're driving."

Her eyes slid to the floor, refusing to meet his. "I was just borrowing it."

"Do you always treat borrowed property like a toy matchbox car?"

"I was careful."

"You sideswiped Gladys."

"Who's Gladys?"

"The SUV you sideswiped—*my* SUV." Actually, it belonged to the King's Army. And technically, Tor was more possessive about the vehicles, since he put in the time and effort to keep them running. And he f-ing named them, so he had more claim to them than anyone else. But close enough.

"Yeah, sorry—I forgot about that—"

"And the bullet holes." He waited, and when she wouldn't meet his eyes, his impatience jumped a few degrees. "And the bloodstains; I bet Bert won't be too happy about those."

She stubbornly refused to respond to his needling.

"Why are you here, Hadley?"

"Can I please go? You don't have any right to hold me. You're not the RCMP." She was bluffing; he could tell by the way she kept darting her eyes to the side. She had no idea who he was.

Keltti had confirmed that she'd shown up by chance, appearing to be a random good Samaritan; that it was nothing more than a coincidence. Yet, this good Samaritan happened to be driving a stolen car. And didn't need directions to Bloddrikker Castle. And didn't carry ID. Totally fishy.

So, who the hell was she?

As long as she wasn't a threat, and he didn't think she was, then he had to let her go. Sunset was coming, and he'd volunteered to take Stu's shift for the night. He shoved his chair back and opened the door with a theatrical wave. "Okay, you're free to go."

She jumped up and peered into the hall suspiciously.

"Your car is this way." He started down the hall that would take them to the parkade and stopped when he realized she was still standing where he'd left her, looking warily between him and the stretch of hall that led in the opposite direction. "No tricks. Just trying to get you out of here so I can get back to work." If he'd wanted to kill her, she'd already be dead.

Apparently, she saw the logic in that because she followed without any further protest.

"So, are you guys like, mercenaries then?" she asked.

Kye raised his eyebrows innocently, and she gave his

weapons harness a pointed look. He could have made up a story to explain away the unorthodox things she'd seen, but just shrugged instead. She'd kept her answers vague, so he would, too.

The stolen car was waiting for her, neatly parked between Naiomi and Sabrina, looking slightly worse for wear with it's battered front fender and bullet holes. After a thorough search, it had been declared clean of any bugs or explosives.

Hadley jumped into the front seat, and the engine turned over with a roar. She drove away without looking back.

Kye watched the taillights until they were out of sight. Something was nagging at the back of his thoughts. It took him a minute to realize what was bugging him—he'd personally searched the car, her bag, and her person and he hadn't found any keys.

So how the hell had she driven away so fast?

CHAPTER 15

Keltti had listened patiently while Stu was questioned by Arvid and Captain Vernar, but now she could see his strength was fading so she diplomatically shuffled them out, reminding them that her patient needed rest so he could heal. She threw the deadbolt, guaranteeing that they'd have some privacy.

Stu had already fallen into a light sleep by the time she turned back to him, so she quickly stripped out of her clothes and tossed them into a nearby garbage. The white shirt and bra would never be white again, and the denim skirt was thick with dried blood and goo. Her panties were possibly salvageable, so she quickly washed them in the bathroom sink and hung them on the back of the door.

The infirmary shower wasn't much, but the hot water felt heavenly and she was grateful there was shampoo and conditioner in the small stall. She scrubbed quickly, wanting to get back to Stu.

Finally, dressed in green medical scrubs, her wet hair towel-dried and finger-combed, she let her fingers trail across his face to his lips. The ripped clothing and dried blood did nothing to hide the deadly predator this male truly was. He opened his eyes, and he put his hand over hers when she would have pulled away, trapping her where she was.

She had almost lost him. Nearly lost this amazing, stubborn, brave male. He'd put his own life in danger, just to protect hers. A tear ran down her face, but she didn't bother to acknowledge it. She had no idea when she'd come to care so much for him. It didn't matter when. She was falling for this Vampire and it terrified her. Might have already fallen for him—but she wasn't ready to consider that possibility yet.

Sensing her turbulent emotions, he levered himself over a few inches with a grunt, and she obligingly climbed onto the bed next to him. Thank the Goddess this place was equipped with gurneys made for soldiers who were six and a half feet tall, with shoulders as wide as a fridge.

She curled her body around his, trying to avoid where he'd been shot. Tears ran freely now, and her shoulders shook with the effort of trying to keep them in.

"Shhh, it's over now." His voice was weaker than she was used to, reminding her that he'd almost died. She gave up on trying to be quiet, and openly sobbed against his healing chest. She cried until her eyes burned and her throat was raw. Her tears mixed with the blood and goo, creating a sticky mess that stuck to her face. Yuck.

"I'm sorry," he whispered against her wet hair.

"What?"

"I didn't protect you. It's my job to keep you safe."

"Look at you! You almost *died!*" She propped herself up on an elbow so she could see his face.

"You really know how to wound a male's ego."

"Are you… *joking?* Seriously, *now* you suddenly develop a sense of humor?" She tried to muster some anger, but all she found was profound gratefulness that he was okay. "Let's get you out of those clothes. And, you need some blood."

"I don't think I'm ready for that much physical activity yet." His eyes glittered with the edges of a smile—the big dummy *was* teasing her.

"I meant… Argh, never mind. Just help me take these off so I can get you cleaned up." *May the Goddess save me from idiot males.*

None of Stu's clothes were worth saving, so Keltti cut

most of them off and left his weapons harness and boots sitting next to the bed. His body hadn't had enough time to finish cleansing the poison from his system, but his wounds had all closed. Despite his protests of being too weak to shower alone, she shoved him under the spray of water and left him to get clean on his own.

Someone had left a tray of sandwiches and fruit outside the infirmary doors, and she gladly filled her empty stomach. Removing the bullet and keeping Stu alive had pushed her healing abilities further than she'd ever tried before, and she felt exhaustion filling every corner of her body. She wondered how long she'd slept; she didn't even know what day it was anymore.

Not long after she heard the water shut off, Stu emerged from the bathroom with a cloud of steam. The standard size towel didn't cover nearly enough of his body, hanging loosely from his hips. It was nearly indecent and might've been funny, if the sight hadn't made her mouth go dry in fascination.

He smirked at her as he settled himself on the freshly made gurney. Darn him and his Vampire senses, he knew exactly what he did to her. The tired lines around his eyes and mouth reminded her that he was still healing, and she managed to keep her hands to herself.

She pulled her hair over her shoulder, exposing her neck and wishing she was wearing something more appropriate than unisex scrubs. "You need blood," she murmured.

He drew her down softly, his large hand warm on the back of her neck. "*Keltti...*" Her name left his lips with reverence, and he gently kissed hers.

Tears pricked the back of her eyelids, and she suddenly knew this is what it felt like to be cherished by a good male. His kiss trailed lower to her jaw, and she felt her body coil in anticipation. "Do it," she whispered against his damp hair.

He slid his fangs in slowly; taking long deep pulls from her vein as her body wound tighter and tighter. He kept one hand firmly under her hair, holding her exactly where he wanted her, while the other slid under the sheets so he could grip his cock. Slowly he pumped himself; his fist matching the rhythm of his mouth on her neck. She tugged the fabric down, her eyes riveted as she watched the head of his cock glisten under the florescent lighting, drops of precum sliding under his firm grip.

The sight of him working himself pushed her over the edge, and she gasped as the orgasm swept through her body. Seconds later, he groaned, and she watched, fascinated as his seed shot out in a hot spurt, followed by another, then another. It hit the blankets, and he groaned again as more landed on the floor. Another groan, and more hit the ceiling. She held her breath, watching until he was finally spent.

Oh, Goddess…

Without thinking, she leaned down and licked the remaining drops from the tip of his cock. It tasted like him, intensely male and—

She screamed, her entire body convulsing as a red-hot poker of pain slammed into her neck. Someone had poured lava down her back. Or maybe she'd been shot. Oh Goddess, it hurt like a million fire ants all chomping down in the same place at the same time. Or maybe a million sharks. Or fire sharks. If there was such a thing. The pain was breaking her mind, making thinking too difficult.

Her body gave out, and she passed into blessed unconsciousness.

Captain Vernar was no fool. In his line of work, fool was just another word for dead.

He kept his face impassive as he studied the male before him.

Dark brown hair in need of a cut, eyes that were a dark blue with enough intelligence to worry Vernar, and the edge of a tattoo that disappeared down the man's chest. He wore faded jeans and a plain white shirt; all typical for most humans. The well-worn boots were a bit of a surprise, a good quality tactical style that the human armies preferred. His bomber style jacket was faded black leather and looked ordinary, but Vernar could smell the gunpowder and steel it was concealing.

The human had shown up at the front gates, demanding an audience with the King. Which had sent off a hell of a lot of warning bells.

The guy knew that they were ruled by a King, but not enough to know that he was on the other side of the globe. Vamp culture wasn't exactly well-known; his kind preferred to keep their affairs private. Tor and Ranvald had picked him up at the main gate and brought him straight to the underground garage. Official guests were admitted through the main lobby, but this guy was a wild card, so full security protocols were followed.

"You're wasting time. I need to speak with the King."

"We'll get to that, but first you can go ahead and hand over your weapons."

The male paused, sizing up Vernar and the two soldiers that flanked him; probably considering the odds of making it out of there alive if he decided to start something that he couldn't finish. Eventually he reached a decision and nodded once before handing over two semi-autos from his shoulder holster, two silver daggers strapped to his forearms, a stiletto from his boot, and five throwing knives from somewhere in the vicinity of his waistband. Ranvald let out an appreciative whistle once all the hardware was handed over.

A quick pat down, a short ride in the elevator, and they were seated in the interrogation room, with Tor and Ranvald acting as sentries in the hall.

"How did you find us?"

"I asked around."

"Bullshit." Vernar cracked an arrogant smile; this asshat thought he was going to sit here and bluff his way thought an interrogation.

The male sighed, irritably. "You're Captain Vernar of the

King's Army. For a few bucks, the Sucubbi on the corner of first and fifteenth were more than happy to have a chat about who the big players in this part of the country are. And FYI, the glamour only works on humans, so I found your Estate just fine; it's actually somewhat of a beacon with so many Vamps in one location." He leaned back in his chair, the barest hint of a smirk on his lips. The cocky bastard.

Vernar didn't let his shock show, just fired another question at the male. "Who are you?"

"Calder Courtland."

"*What* are you?"

"I'm a Psionic."

"Bullshit."

"You said that already."

"You're human; Psionics don't exist."

"Some would say that Vampires don't exist."

"Touché." He crossed his arms and sat back in his chair, letting silence take over.

"Look, I'm just here for some information. I tracked a woman here two nights ago, and it's imperative that I find her."

"Let me guess, she's in danger and you want to save her."

A muscle in Courtland's jaw ticked. "She's in trouble."

"What kind of trouble?"

Instead of answering, he threw out a question of his own. "Are you aware of TEAM TRUST?"

Now it was Vernar's turn to hesitate. He had no idea what the asshole was talking about, but he didn't like to admit ignorance.

"They're technically a branch of the American Government, but they operate under the radar with little direction. They're full name is Telekinetically Enhanced Agents Mandating Testing and Research of Unknown Supernatural Terrorists." He paused to let that sink in before continuing. "They're hunting Psionics, but have been

146

known to take Shifters, Sirens, Valkyries, and yeah, even Vamps. Basically, anyone who gets in their way."

"Even if I believed you—which I don't—why should I care?"

"Because they're here. Right now. In Calgary."

"Why? Why now?"

"They're after the girl. I need to find her before they do. Any other supernaturals that they come across are just gravy on the side, something for their testing and research lab to cut apart and play with."

"What do they want her for?" Jeez, he was starting to buy into this load of shit.

"She's Psionic; extremely powerful. They'll try to convert her to their side. If she won't go willingly, they'll use torture and brainwashing. They will do whatever it takes to turn her into a tool that they can use."

"And how exactly is this the King's problem?"

"It's everyone's problem! Once they've tracked down all the Psionics, do you think they're just going to stop? They're amassing an army! How long before they realize the benefits to having soldiers with Vampire strength, speed, and healing? Or those that can shift at will? We're all targets."

Vernar mulled over the possibilities, letting different scenarios play out in his head. Hypothetically, this could be a big fucking problem.

The darkness receded in waves, like the tide going out at the beach.

The first thing Keltti became aware of were the nice soft sheets that pillowed her body. They smelled like Stu, and it made her entire body relax, knowing he must be nearby. Her body hurt all over, as if she had been hit by a train.

Stretching made her wince, but it was tolerable. Sitting up slowly, she realized she was in Stu's bedroom. Her borrowed scrubs were tossed on the floor, next to one of the generic hospital blankets. A quick check under the blankets confirmed that, yep, she was naked.

The side of her neck throbbed with a heartbeat of its own. She gently prodded the tender skin; it felt raised like a burn that had scarred. Stu's bite was still there too, a few inches higher and mostly healed.

The sound of male voices drifted through the partially open bedroom door. Stu was out there; she could sense his presence just by concentrating now. It was like a metaphysical rope between them. She gave a tiny experimental tug and immediately felt his shock. And then something like... Approval? Her empathetic talents felt ramped up; but she wasn't getting a thing from whoever else was out there.

"...It happened..."

"...Mating mark... Fucking knew..."

"Lucky son of a..."

There was a solid thump of muscle on muscle and the unmistakable clap of a hand on bare skin—was her big bad Vampire man-hugging another male? The thought made her grin.

The rumble of goodbyes was followed by silence; but she was acutely aware that Stu was still nearby. She could feel his presence getting closer; until he quietly stepped into the room. His face was neutral, but she could read his emotions as easily as her own. Uncertainty and trepidation followed by a tangle of joy and disbelief. And underneath it all was a deep-seated primal satisfaction that can only come with having a Y chromosome.

She patted the bed, and he sat warily, like he was approaching a wounded animal.

"We're mated." It wasn't a question, but she still needed his confirmation.

He nodded, his Adam's apple bobbing as he tried to find the right words. "Yeah... I—I didn't... ah, Sunshine, I'm sorry."

She studied him, watching the colours in his aura flash back and forth. "I'm not. I'm not sorry at all."

Shock flitted through his eyes but was quickly replaced

by a smug male confidence. "You're mine."

"You are such a caveman." She laughed, wondering how this big primitive-minded Vampire was going to fair when she educated him on women's rights.

His eyes darkened, then turned red and he prowled on all fours across the bed towards her. "Say it."

"Say what?" She backed up, suddenly aware that she was still naked with nothing but a sheet between them.

"You're mine. Say it." He stalked even closer, until her back was against the headboard and she had nowhere else to go.

"Stu…" Her pulse skyrocketed, her flight or fight instincts kicking in.

He grabbed her by the ankle and yanked her forward until she was lying on her back. He crawled up her body, his movements smooth like the predator he was. "Say it." The demand wound its way up her spine and sent spikes of pleasure shooting lower.

"I'm… Yours." she whispered, pulling him down into a kiss that said exactly how she felt about being his.

Stu's world settled into place. He felt balanced in a way that he hadn't even known was missing until now. His little Witch, *his mate*, was curled against his side, glowing in a way that only a completely satisfied, well-loved female can manage. Her hair was a wild mess, and her lips were rosy and swollen from his attentions. Her mating mark had settled into a beautiful wreath of flowering vines and branches in earthy green tones. It was permanent now; she was officially stuck with him.

He'd have to invite his father for a visit—he already had questions about the mating bond and wanted to be prepared for whatever might lie ahead. He'd managed to blunder his way though the actual mating, despite his lack of knowledge.

He felt a small amount of guilt at the way things had happened; he'd wanted to give her a thorough claiming once his body had completely healed, drawing out the experience and making it last all night. Who knew the ancient ritual didn't care itself how it happened, so long as he took her blood and she took his seed?

Calder walked along the empty highway, his frustration an ugly, festering emotion that snaked through his chest and threatened to cloud his judgement. He'd been chasing Hadley for weeks; every time he got close, she'd slip through his grasp. He had to find her before TRUST did.

His rental car was waiting for him right where he'd left it, on the side of the road, hidden between the thick pine trees.

The Vampires hadn't provided the answers he'd been hoping for. They'd denied any knowledge of Hadley, and made it clear they weren't concerned about TRUST. The sheer arrogance and stupidity made him want to put his fist through their overly confident faces. Still, he wasn't stupid. No reason to piss off an entire contingent of well trained, experienced fighters. He had no doubts who'd win that particular fight.

He'd need to update his superiors soon; he could only delay for so long before they decided he was no longer the right man for the job. Somewhere between Broken Arrow, Oklahoma, and Calgary, Hadley had become more than just another assignment. He still hadn't been able to catch up to her in person, yet she'd become more than just a photo in a manila folder.

Without a fresh lead or any idea of where to start looking, Calder started the car and headed back towards the city. His prey had evaded him long enough; her days on the run were numbered. She just hadn't realized it yet.

Wearing yet another set of borrowed scrubs from the infirmary, Keltti skipped lightly down the stairs into the parking garage. Her sandals smacked the pavement, leaving loud slaps echoing in the large space. The straps were stained with blood and goo, and she planned to toss them into the nearest garbage as soon as she got home.

Using borrowed keys for Gladys—with Kye's permission, of course—Keltti climbed into the bulky SUV and started the engine. Darn Vampires with their massive height. She couldn't even reach the pedals until she moved the seat forward eight or nine inches. Excruciatingly loud music, belonging to a genre that she couldn't even identify, blared out of the speakers until she found the volume control. *Enough of that noise*, she though as she spun the dial until something more enjoyable came on.

"Okay, Gladys, how about we go for a drive?" Not expecting an answer, she put the vehicle into drive and pulled out of the lot.

The highway was deserted, with early morning mist hanging in the lower lying areas. It was beautiful and spooky. And just like her mate, it would disappear with the rising of the sun.

Her *mate*. Just thinking the words made her smile. He was nothing like she'd imagined a mate would be—yet, he was everything she'd ever wanted.

Bright lights in her rear-view mirror momentarily blinded her. She squinted, her eyes dancing with black spots for a moment before her vision returned. Immediately she saw a dark vehicle sitting in the middle of the highway, and she slammed on her breaks.

Gladys skidded for several seconds before the tires were able to grip the road and she cranked the wheel towards the ditch to avoid a collision. The wheel jerked as she hit the shoulder of the road, and she was thrown against the seatbelt. It bit into her shoulder until her vehicle came to a stop against a fencepost, the airbags on both sides deploying with a *bang!*

Oh, Goddess… Her thoughts fought to catch up to the present and she fumbled with her seatbelt release. She got the door open and lurched out into the tall grass on her hands and knees. Heavy footsteps crunched in the gravel, and she looked up to see thick black boots walking towards her. Four pairs, if her vision wasn't compromised by the crash.

"You two, grab her." The voice was arrogant and nasal, and made goosebumps rise on her arms. The smell of unwashed bodies made bile rise in her throat. All four were human, which was a small blessing. She'd take what she could at this point.

Cold hands grabbed her by both arms, pulling her to her feet. "So, this is the healer that the Doc is so obsessed with procuring." The male wasn't impressed, contempt dripping from his voice like something wet and slimy. He looked to be in his thirties, and he wore black cargo pants with a matching shirt and boots. His hair was plain brown, cut in a standard military style which nearly hid the grey streaks.

He grabbed her chin and forced her head back to examine her like a thoroughbred with dubious papers. She struggled to back away, but the two holding her were extremely strong for humans.

"Thane, come here." The male behind him stepped forward, tossing his long greasy blonde hair nervously over his shoulder. His plaid shirt was reminiscent of a nineties grunge band and needed a good wash. The majority of the body odor that Keltti had noticed earlier was coming from him.

In one smooth motion, the first male pulled a knife and stabbed the blonde in stomach. She let out a startled gasp at the exact same time as he did. The color drained from his face, and he stumbled back holding his belly before falling on his butt in the weeds.

"Okay, Witch, prove your worth." The leader gestured with a flourish at the male laying on the ground.

The two males holding her up tossed her forward, and she landed in the grass next to the injured human. His high-pitched squeals sent shivers through her body, making her arms shake as she tried to crawl closer.

"Heal him. Now." He gestured with his knife, tiny splatters of blood disappearing into the grass. There was no missing the implied threat that she would be next if she didn't obey.

They weren't asking her to do anything terrible. She could do this; healing was what she did.

The male flinched away from her and she had to scoot closer to be able to reach him. She touched his hand and let the healing light in her free. It eagerly ran down his arm, stopping to wrap itself around the track marks under his shirt, before continuing towards the stab wound.

There wasn't much internal damage, none of his major organs had been nicked. The flesh mended easily, and his body wouldn't take long to replenish the lost blood. She pulled her hand away, shutting down the connection. Drugs had tainted every part of the male, and she felt vaguely ill from the contact.

Still whimpering, he lifted his shirt and tenderly probed the healed skin.

"Well, well... Nicely done," the leader mused, his sharp eyes held grudging approval. "Take her."

The two males built like brick walls advanced on her, one holding a plastic zip-tie. They matched from their identical camo shirts, right down to their faded blue jeans and spiked black hair.

Scrambling to her feet, she lurched towards the forest. The closest one lunged for her and his big fingers brushed her arm as she ducked and continued running. The forest closed around her, blocking out the morning sun and making it difficult to see. The bushes and scrub were dense and scraped at her arms and face as she ran blindly, not caring where she was going as long it put her further from her pursuers. More than once she bounced off a tree trunk and fell.

She didn't know how many of the humans had followed her. The two bruisers weren't far behind; she could hear them plowing through the undergrowth like bulldozers. She was grateful for the warm weather that had kept the leaves on the trees, since they helped shield her from her hunters.

The scrubs she wore had no pockets. Why hadn't she thought to bring her cell? The battery was dead, and she'd left it in the infirmary bathroom when she'd showered. She was truly on her own—at least until the sun went down. Her mating mark heated and tingled; she knew Stu would come for her. But that wouldn't be for hours. She just needed to survive until then.

She swallowed a scream when her foot met air and her body tipped forward, instinctively clutching at the branches around her. Gravity pulled her downhill, and she threw her arms up to protect her head and face. She rolled, smacking into smaller tree trunks that felt like baseball bats against her back and ribs. When she finally reached the bottom of the ravine, her head spun and made the ground beneath her feel like it was tilting back and forth.

Spitting out leaves and dirt, she got to her knees.

Something solid and heavy smacked her in the back of the head and she felt the bones in her cheek crack as her face hit the rocky ground. Then she couldn't feel anything at all.

CHAPTER 16

Sunset loomed over the mountains in the distance. Bloddrikker Castle was slowly becoming more active as soldiers prepared for the night.

"Are you sure you don't want me to take your shift again? It *is* your first night as a mated male; don't you have duties to preform?" Kye waggled his silver eyebrows suggestively and Stu couldn't control the low growl that escaped his chest.

"Fuck off. Don't talk about my mate. Don't even think about her."

The younger Vamp held up his hands in mock-surrender and turned to leave. "Stay safe, you lucky mated bastard. Oh, and have her return the keys to Gladys when she get's a second."

Stu's hand froze on the dagger he was strapping on, his entire body going still. "My mate took a vehicle out?" He was dimly aware that his eyes had turned red.

"Whoa, Stu—she went home to get some clothes and things this morning. She's not back yet?" Kye's voice stayed calm, but anxiety caused his muscles to tense beneath the ivory sweater he wore.

Opening his mind and body to the mating bond, Stu cast out mental feelers, quickly searching the castle and grounds for any sign of his Witch. Nothing. Panic threatened to set in, and he expanded his search with the same result.

Icy fingers of fear slid down his spine.

She was gone.

It took less than ten minutes for every available soldier to amass in the Operations room.

Every one of the males who gathered had worked with her, had vowed to protect her, and had been healed by her. She'd managed to penetrate their tight bond of brotherhood and insert herself into their affections, effectively wrapping them around her little finger.

Word of her newly mated status quickly spread, and the ante rose exponentially. Mated females were rare and should be kept safe at all costs. Every male here would willingly give his life for hers. Some of the younger males had only heard of the mating bond in stories and legends—any mated females in the area were kept locked away at home by their males. Rightfully so. He'd be having a long talk with his little Witch about that as soon as he found her.

"I got a ping on Gladys! Thirty kilometers east of here." Kye tapped furiously on his keyboard, relaying info as it became available. "She left just before oh-seven-hundred, traveling towards the city, then eighteen minutes later the airbags deployed and there was a front-end collision. She hasn't moved since."

Stu was already halfway to the door when Kye tossed him a set of keys. "Take Miranda." Behind him, Arvid caught another set with instructions to take Naiomi. Vernar and Ros were close behind, their boots pounding the cement steps as they hit the parking garage.

They made it to the crash site in less than seven minutes thanks to Tor's handywork beneath the hood of the vehicles. The speed governors were long gone, and they had fucking redlined it the entire way.

Gladys sat with her front end twisted in a barb-wire fence. Twin tracks in the tall grass led back to where she had left the road.

The scent of his mate's blood lingered in the air, coppery and sweet, mingling with the fresh pine air. Rage and determination filled him, his hands palming his guns, eager to shoot something. The raw primal need to draw blood was ancient, and as instinctive to a bonded male as breathing.

Aside from the collapsed airbags, nothing was out of place in the otherwise clean vehicle. Keltti's house keys sat abandoned in the cup holder and he scooped them up and tucked them safely into his pocket, refusing to leave even that one tiny bit of his mate's life behind.

A few feet from the SUV, Stu kneeled next to a trampled patch of grass the size of a body. Blood had soaked into the dirt—human blood. *Good girl.* She'd fought back and injured at least one of her attackers.

"I've got tracks!" Sarge called from the tree line.

Keltti woke with a pounding headache. Opening her eyes, she caught a glimpse of a grey steel wall, before bright white flashes of light exploded in her head and her vision went black.

Pain was something she was used to. As the King's official healer, she had spent a fair bit of her time with wounded soldiers and her empathetic abilities made their pain hers. But this was a whole new world of hurt for her. Like an entire army of elephants was stampeding back and forth in her head. In tap shoes. With their boom-boxes cranked up, balanced on their shoulders. *Just like in the cartoons...*

The thought almost made her smile—but instead she rolled onto her side and threw up. Her stomach gave its best effort, but nothing came out aside from a lot of retching and gasping noises.

She fell back, exhausted.

Something cool and wet brushed across her face, and she tried to slap it away but even her arms weren't cooperating.

"Shhh. Go back to sleep." a woman's voice soothed, light and musical.

That was a bad idea; she probably had a concussion and should stay awake. The beating in her head made the decision for her, and she sank into welcome unconsciousness.

Frustrated beyond fucking belief, Stu waited impatiently for an update from Operations. The whole concept of doing nothing went against every instinct he had. His arms flexed and bunched beneath his leather coat, needing to tear something apart.

He'd easily tracked his mates trail through the forest; every drop of her spilt blood pushing his bloodlust higher and higher. Two kilometers later, the trail had ended at the bottom of a dried-up river bed. Her scent had lingered on the dead leaves littering the ground. She must have laid there for some time.

The scent of human males had accompanied her; and one of the two sets of large footprints had bit deeper into the ground as they'd backtracked out of the woods. She'd been carried out, and the thought of some fucking humans' filthy hands on his mate had made him see red. He'd put his fist through the trunk of a poplar; blood from his broken knuckles dripped onto the same ground where his Witch had laid in her own blood.

Some fucking mate he was. Less than a day, and he'd already failed to protect her.

"I've got her cell." Adrianus barrelled into the Operations room, and handed it over to Stu. "It was in the infirmary."

He desperately pushed the small device's buttons, hoping it would lead him to his mate. "It's dead!" His growl had the younger Vampire backing away with wide eyes.

Stu fought the urge to smash the useless piece of plastic against the wall, tossing it to Kye instead. Maybe he could get it to tell them something beneficial.

He pivoted, ready to resume his pacing, when a stab of pain lanced through his head. It was sharper than a knife and tasted like his little Witch.

Keltti! He frantically grasped at the link between them, mentally feeding all his power into the fragile connection between them. It was full of confusion and agony and the disorientation was so strong it made the castle spin around him. It lasted for about thirty seconds, and then faded away between one breath and the next.

He realized Tor was holding his elbow; the male had probably kept him from falling on his ass. The entire room had gone quiet and everyone was staring at him and he belatedly realized that he hadn't been shouting only in his head.

"I felt her." His voice cracked and he couldn't even give a shit that he sounded like a wuss. "She's hurt. And weak."

"But she's alive?" Arvid spoke the words that they'd all been thinking since leaving the crash site.

"Yeah, but I think she's unconscious. Maybe drugged."

"Could you tell where she was?"

"West. Maybe a bit north, definitely west."

"You can tell that from the mating bond?"

"Yeah." He didn't miss the look of envy his brothers exchanged. Smothering his smug male pride, he tried to focus on what Kye was saying.

"Stu, can you tell how far away she is?"

"No. The link was weak—maybe because she's injured, maybe she's too far?" Fuck, he had no idea what the rules were.

Kye spread a map across the table and tapped the paper with his index finger. "We're here. So, she's got to be somewhere in this area." The pie-shaped section of the map dauntingly covered a large portion of natural forest before reaching the Rocky Mountains. It would take weeks to search that much rugged terrain; but Stu wasn't willing to sit around waiting for the mating bond to lead him to his missing mate. If she was sedated, she could be unable to reach him indefinitely.

"We need to get out there." He needed to fucking *do* something. Now. He had to get out there and find her. He was wasting precious time standing here talking about it.

Thankfully, Vernar had picked up on his restlessness and

159

started dividing the map into a grid, giving each two-man team a section to search. He was the King's best tracker, so Stu didn't question his methods, trusting him explicitly.

Kye tossed him a set of keys, and Stu was out the door before anyone could stop him.

CHAPTER 17

Simon woke to someone knocking on his door.

The room was pitch black, and a quick tap on his watch showed it was just after four in the morning. Whoever was outside his suite had better have a damn good reason for waking him at such an early hour.

He pulled on a pair of boxers before swinging the heavy door open.

Darrell, his second in command, waited tensely in the hall. "Alpha," he acknowledged his leader with a quick nod.

"It's early Darrell; what do you need?" He was careful to keep his irritation in check; the male wouldn't be here if it wasn't urgent.

"The Vampires are requesting our assistance, sir."

Simon felt his eyebrows involuntarily rising. "The *Vampires*?"

"Yes, sir, the King's Army." *What the hell was going on?*

"The *King's Army*?" Jeez, he sounded like a broken record. "And quit with the sir crap."

"They've asked for our best trackers," He paused so they could both smirk; every single Wolf in his Pack was a better tracker than any Vampire would ever be. "And they want us to take over for their men once the sun rises."

"What are they tracking?" It must be something big if they were willing to call upon his Pack for help.

"Their healer has been kidnapped."

His heart dropped into his stomach as shock and dread washed over him. "Keltti?"

"Yes, sir."

He stalked to his closet and randomly started to pull clothes on while his mind worked furiously, making a mental list of his most trusted Wolves and what equipment they might need.

"How many Wolves can we spare?"

"Twelve to fourteen, if we keep just a skeleton crew on security."

"Do it. Put the compound on lock down; no one leaves." Someone had enough balls to kidnap the King's healer, and until he found out who it was, he wasn't taking any chances with the Dark Shadow Pack. The women and children would make easy targets outside the safety of the compound.

What the hell was going on? He'd bet it had something to do with the black-haired Vampire from the bar a few nights ago. He'd claimed to be Keltti's mate. It was a ridiculous notion; she had clearly wanted nothing to do with him.

Damn, he shouldn't have let her leave with him. As a friend of the Pack, she was under his protection. Instead of keeping her safe, he'd trusted the soldiers to take care of her. He hadn't wanted to let his Wolves get pulled into a fight with the Vampires. Diplomacy at it's fucking finest. It would have been one hell of a fight too. But now Keltti was paying for his mistake.

"We leave in twenty minutes." Trusting Darrell to take care of the details, he walked out the door towards his sister's suite.

She wasn't part of his security team, but she was an amazing tracker. There was no point in wasting time arguing with her to stay home; he knew she'd take this personally and would insist on joining him. He could understand that. This was personal for him too.

Since the search efforts for Keltti had started, Stu had felt the mating bond stir twice. Both times, it had been a slow dimmed version of what it should be and lasted only a few seconds. The first time he'd mentally demanded that she answer him; the second time he'd begged. She hadn't answered him either time.

The sun would rise in just over an hour; he was running out of time.

He stepped out of the dense underbrush onto a small dirt road, with Arvid only a few steps behind. His normally chatty brother-in-arms had remained unusually quiet for the duration of their slog through nature, and for that, Stu was grateful.

A hundred yards down the road, Adrianus waited in an idling SUV, with his heavy metal music pumping through the air. He pushed his hair back nervously and stepped on the gas once both soldiers were seated. Glancing warily in the rear-view mirror, he was oddly anxious. "About time. The sun's going to be up soon." Ahh… That's what was eating at the kid. Younger Vamps were more sensitive to the sun—he was probably shitting himself at being out so close to sunrise.

They stopped to pick up Sarge and Ros ten kilometers down the road, and then rode in tense silence down the rutted worn road. Eventually, they pulled up next to a mammoth-sized RV parked as far off the road as possible. It said "Sunthief" on the side, and had the distinct look of a vehicle made in the early nineties.

"What the hell is *that*?" Arvid muttered under his breath as they approached the boxy metal beast.

Tor stepped out of the side door, and grinned. "She's a thirty-six-foot, all terrain sunthief M37, with a 12.9-liter pro-amp MX-13 under the hood. Eighteen hundred and fifty pounds of torque. I call her Mabel." His voice was coarse and efficient as he rattled off the specs.

"Why the hell would you put a semi engine in a hunk of junk like this?" Adrianus hadn't been with them long, and Tor was a hard nut to crack, so he truly had no idea how talented Tor was off the battlefield. His ability to modify anything with four wheels and an engine was legendary, and it had saved their bacon on too many occasions to count. Most of their combat was hand-to-hand, but vehicles were a necessity to get there in the first place.

Ros smacked Adrian in the back of the head and followed Tor into his newest construction.

The entire RV had been gutted. Instead of the typically quaint camping unit for families with a tiny kitchen, even smaller bathroom, and sleeping arrangements of the fold-up variety, Mabel boasted a large refrigerator, with floor to ceiling glass doors, a high-tech operations wall with multiple LED screens, and a wall of bunks that were wide enough to accommodate the shoulders of every male present.

The driver's seat was behind a small door that, when shut, would keep the cabin completely separate.

"The walls are triple-paned steel, completely bulletproof. The windows are bulletproof glass, with metal shutters that secure here." He demonstrated on the nearest window. "Totally sun proof."

Even Stu had to admit he was impressed. It saved them from having to head back to the castle, which would waste valuable minutes in getting back here once the sun was down again.

The sound of multiple vehicles arriving had everyone exiting with preternatural speed, their weapons ready as they formed an attack formation.

He caught the scent of Werewolves, even before the occupants exited the two large cargo vans.

Sarge lowered his guns first, and motioned for everyone else to do the same. That was fine with Stu—he didn't need his guns to kick their asses. It would be more fun with his bare hands.

"Captain Vernar." The Alpha acknowledged Sarge with a nod, his Wolves taking a protective stance behind him. A few melted into the shadows of the forest and disappeared. Probably surveying the area. Or circling around to attack from behind.

"Alpha, thank you for coming on such short notice."

What the *hell?* Sarge had *invited* these asshats here?

"Call me Simon. I've read the dossier Kyenel sent over. Anything else I should know before we head out?"

"No fucking way—" Stu started forward, intent on smashing the smug smile off his pretty face.

"Stukavarius! At ease soldier!" Stu stopped dead in his tracks, unable to disobey a direct command from his Captain. "We're out of options. These guys can do a lot of the leg work while the sun is up. It's our best shot at getting her back."

Damn it all to hell, Sarge was right. And didn't that just piss him off even more.

"How do we know these bastards aren't involved?"

"Keltti is a friend of the Dark Shadow Pack, and under my protection. I *will* bring her back. Now that you've had the last—" Simon looked pointedly at his watch, "twenty-three hours to find her, but haven't, it's our turn." He purposefully started stripping down, and immediately the Wolves behind him followed suit.

Tor and Sarge each grabbed one of Stu's biceps as he lunged for the Alpha. No fucking *way* was a naked male getting anywhere near his mate—especially *this* naked male.

There was some discussion of the four-lettered variety before Stu was finally released.

"We'll be in contact by cell once an hour. Kye has the numbers for my men who will be on foot." He deposited his neatly folded clothes into a duffel bag that was being passed between the naked males.

The back of Stu's neck tingled, letting him know the sun was already cresting the horizon and would make its way through the overhead leaves in a matter of minutes.

"I'll need something that carries Keltti's scent; some of my Wolves have never had the pleasure of meeting her." Stu's hands ached from resisting the urge to break every single one of the asshole's perfect teeth.

Stu pulled her house keys out of his pocket and tossed them across the road to the Alpha. Four of the males took turns sniffing them, then threw them back before noiselessly stepping into the forest.

Fucking Werewolves.

The bright white shards of pain in Keltti's head had downgraded to tiny strikes of lightning. Her stomach no longer revolted, and she wasn't quite as dizzy, as long as she laid perfectly still.

Her right eye refused to open, and her cheek throbbed in time with her heartbeat. Wincing from the contact, she forced her fingers to catalog the extent of her injuries. Her face was swollen beyond recognition; there was a knot on the back of her head that had crusted over with blood; her left shoulder was bruised all the way down her collarbone onto her right breast; and her arms and feet were crisscrossed with multiple scratches of varying depths.

Someone had attempted to clean her up by washing away some of the dirt and blood. Her ugly green scrubs were ripped and stained with grime, but at least she was still dressed.

A quick scan with her second-sight let her know there were two other people in the room with her.

"You're awake." She recognized the woman's voice from one of her more lucid moments earlier.

"Mmm... Hmm..." was all Keltti could manage to get out; her throat was parched like the inside of a chimney that hadn't been cleaned in twenty years.

"Here's some water; drink slow." An arm helped her to sit up. The plastic bottle was room temperature when it touched her lips, and the water felt like heaven on her dry tongue.

Keltti could see the female now, kneeling next to the cot that she was lying on. The female's face was oval shaped, and her nose slightly turned up at the end, making her beautiful in a classic sort of way. Hair, the color of fresh snow, ran in long waves down her back. Her clothes were stylish, but wrinkled as if she'd been wearing them for more than a day.

"Are you feeling better?"

"Honestly, not much. Where are we?" Keeping her good eye open, she scanned the room.

They were in some sort of cage with three metal walls and a glass one. The floor and ceiling were solid rock that had obviously been crudely dug. Two more metal bunks were against another wall and were stacked one on top of the other. A dark-haired woman sat on the top bunk, watching Keltti with an empty look on her face.

Both women looked to be in their twenties, but you couldn't judge a supernatural's age by his or her physical appearance. The blonde was obviously a Nymph, but Keltti wasn't sure about the second.

"I don't know. We woke up here, like you did. I'm Karina and that's Lysette."

"Keltti Callinwood. How long have you been here?"

"I've been here two months, but Lysette was a couple months longer, give or take."

"How long was I—"

Keltt! Sunshine? She grimaced as Stu's voice filled her head, as loud and as unexpected as a gun shot.

Ow! Stu? Hope wared with irritation at the mental intrusion.

Where are you? Are you hurt? Tell me where you are. I'm coming to get you. Did they hurt you? I'll kill every one of—

Stop talking! Goddess, her head was going to explode. *I'm okay, it's probably just a concussion.*

She could feel the stillness settle over him, the tightly leashed rage that burned beneath his calm words. *Who hurt you?*

I don't know. There were four of them. They were working for someone... Her head ached as she thought back. *Doc? A Doctor?*

Son of a... She could feel his disgust, feel him fighting to hide it from her.

Who is he?

I don't know. I'll deal with him; just tell me where you are.

I don't know. In a cage, the floor and ceiling are rock. It's cold; probably underground.

"Keltti?" Karina's voice interrupted her thoughts, and she sounded worried.

Give me a minute.

"Sorry?" It was a little disorienting to switch her attention back to the Nymph.

"Are you okay? You just spaced out on us."

"I'm fine. Just thinking." She wasn't ready to trust these women yet; she wouldn't put it past her captors to plant a mole in here with her.

Standing on shaky legs, she wobbled over to the metal door set in the glass wall. As she suspected, it was locked. The glass was an inch thick, probably bulletproof. Metal rivets marched across the metal walls in neat little rows every four feet. They were most likely reinforcing seams that had been welded together. No chance of escape there—at least, not without one heck of a chisel and crowbar. And maybe some dynamite.

The bunks were screwed directly into the walls, so there was no possibility of using the bedframes to pry open the door. The back corner of the room was divided off with frosted glass walls, hiding a small toilet and sink. The accommodations were crude, and she found it interesting that they had indoor plumbing at all. This place had obviously been thought out ahead of time.

Sunshine?

I'm still here.

Footsteps approached, and Karina and Lysette visibly flinched and moved further from the door. A male came into view carrying a cafeteria tray. Keltti recognized him as the human she had healed earlier that day. Or yesterday. Or whatever day it was that she'd crashed the SUV and been abducted.

Pulling on strength she hoped she had, she lowered her mental shields and sought him out with her second sight.

His aura was bright and glowed with health. Obviously, he hadn't had a chance to imbibe in any drugs since she'd seen him last. The bloody flannel shirt and ripped jeans had been replaced with slightly cleaner similar versions, but he still hadn't showered. Eww.

His gaze skittered across her cellmates before landing shyly on Keltti. "Hi. You're awake."

"Thane." She was surprised she remembered his name. And really, she had no idea what else to say.

"Are you okay? I brought you some cereal." Guilt swirled through his aura, an ugly pea green color that made her queasy to watch. She struggled to put her shields back in place. "All we have is wheatie bites. I hope that's okay…"

He bent down and set the tray on the floor so he could select one of a dozen keys on a large ring that he pulled out of his pocket. Inserting it in a lock close to the floor until it clicked, he slid the bottom panel of the door open. It was only six inches high, just tall enough to slide the food under. Not big enough for a fully grown female to escape through. He was careful to lock it once he was done, sliding nervous glances at the women until it was secure.

Jamming his hands into his pockets, he lingered awkwardly but didn't say anything.

"Thank you, Thane," she murmured. His smile was brief and boyish before he shuffled away.

Keltti lifted the tray and carried it back to where Karina was sitting. The Nymph absently accepted the cardboard bowl of soggy cereal and a plastic spoon. "He likes you." she mused.

"Yeah, I healed him when he was stabbed." That would be enough to make any human grateful. Her head hurt, so she didn't bother going into details.

Keltti? Stu's worry shot down the bonding link, startling her with its intensity.

I'm okay. Just tired and my face hurts.
Can you heal it?
I don't have enough energy.

She staggered, her knees giving out as pure energy punched into her body, filling her with power while knocking her on her butt. Literally. Her vision wavered, while bright lights that only she could see filled the room. Warmth infused her aching body, smoothing over the jagged nerve endings and soothing the pain away. Healing light—*her* healing light—surrounded her body, caressing it one injury at a time. It was incredibly intimate, and she made a sound that was usually for Stu's ears alone.

"What the *hell*?" Keltti opened her eyes to see both females staring in shock at her.

What happened?

I don't know—I just thought of you...

She felt energized, like he was standing right next to her, feeding her his power. It even smelled like him, all leather and spicy male.

"Your face is better. How did you do that?" Awe tinted Karina's voice.

"Honestly, I have no idea." They sat in silence for a few moments, each lost in their own thoughts.

Eventually, Keltti picked up her uneaten meal and gestured at the others to do the same. "Eat up, ladies. I have a feeling we're going to need our strength once the sun goes down."

"Why?"

"Because I'm not waiting around for someone to come get us. We're going to rescue ourselves."

Stu could feel her determination to act, to take matters into her own hands. To protect him and his brothers from harm.

No! Sunshine, just wait for me—I'll be there as soon as I can. It was only about ten in the morning—way too many fucking hours before sunset.

Her thoughts were hidden from him behind shields that were stronger and thicker than any armour. He could sense her concentration as she tried furiously to find a way out of the danger she was in.

There are other women here. Two in my cell, maybe more. There aren't many guards—

No! Stay where you are, and I'll come get you!

Are you telling me what to do? There was a dark undercurrent to her words.

Damn straight I am! You're my mate and I'll do what I have to keep you safe!

That's not how this works. And just like that, she shut him out again. He could still feel the bond connecting them, but it was the equivalent of a phone's dial tone instead of an open conversation. How dare she! It was his duty, his honor to protect her.

He'd done a real bang-up job so far, though; it was no wonder she didn't trust him to take care of her.

Someone really needed to write a manual on this shit. Stu was getting so fucking sick of trying to figure it out on his own.

CHAPTER 18

Information was the key to good planning. So Keltti gathered as much as she could while plotting her escape. She wasn't stupid—she knew that the King's Army would be a big part of it, with her mate being the largest factor of all. For now, she pushed all thoughts of him out of her mind so that she could concentrate.

Karina answered question after question, while Lysette only offered clipped, one-word answers when she had to. According to the Nymph, the humans were just grunt labour, hired to do the dirty work by a Vamp named Kallikan. He was hunting females of different supernatural breeds as well as humans, capturing them alive and bringing them here.

"They keep the humans in the lab. They've done things to them. I think… I think they're trying to turn them into Vamps." Her large violet eyes held fear and sadness. Keltti reinforced her shields to block the onslaught of strong emotions.

"That's not possible. Vamps are born, not turned like in the movies."

"I heard them talking about it when they were taking my blood. They're draining the women and replacing it with our blood."

"Why on Earth would they do that? It's senseless." If this Kallikan was a Vampire, he'd know it wasn't possible to turn a human into a Vamp, any more than you could turn a cat into a dog.

The familiar shuffle of Thane's footsteps sounded as he approached the glass wall. He'd showered sometime in the last few hours, and his hair was blonder now that it wasn't so greasy. It looked as though he had scrubbed himself with sandpaper. Pink colored his face, making the pockmarks stand out in stark contrast. His standard uniform of worn plaid and ripped denim was wrinkled, but it was clean.

"Hi, Keltti." He spoke hesitantly, quickly glancing away from the stink-eye that the other two females were shooting at him. "I brought you some lunch. I'm not much of a cook, but you'll need your strength to see the Doc tonight."

Icy cold dread slid down Keltti's back, and she fought to keep her voice neutral. "Oh? What's happening tonight?"

"Kallikan wants to be there, so Doc has to wait until he arrives, after the sun goes down. They've never had a Witch before. Don't worry; they'll probably just take your blood. I can bring you some cookies or juice after you're done, if you want?" He sounded hopeful, eager to please her.

"Sure, that would be great." She figured she had better not burn any bridges that she might need in the future, so she tried to paste a genuine looking smile on her face to match the words. But seriously, there's no way she was going to let someone drain her blood for some evil science experiment. She planned to be long gone by the time the sun went down.

Thane slid a food tray under the door, before locking it and giving her one last cautious smile. Once he was gone, some of the tension drained from Karina's body.

"That's so messed up. Did you cast a love-spell on him or something?" she asked.

"Of course not. I just heal; spells aren't really my thing." She examined the offerings he had left: a bowl of ripple chips, three apples, and three bottles of water. Different options slid through her mind, and a plan started to form.

"Okay ladies, we need to be gone before sunset. *Before* those psychopaths try anything stupid." Like taking her blood, which her mate would easily argue was his. And he didn't like to share.

"I need you ready to run. So, who needs some healing magic?" She held up her hands and waggled her fingers with a grin.

Stu glared at the ceiling of the massive RV. If his eyes had lasers, there'd be a big fucking hole in Mabel's roof. And he'd be fucking dead. Burnt to a crisp by the sun as she slowly crept across the sky, agonizingly slow, minute by minute, bringing them that much closer to protective darkness. Not fucking soon enough.

The Captain had confined Stu to his bunk after his restless pacing had stretched Sarge's last bit of patience. Or, possibly it was due to the fist that Stu had put through one of the LED monitors in a bought of frustration. Who knew? Really, who cared?

The Wolves had called after finding the main entrance to some kind of underground bunker. And then again after finding a separate entrance that served as a back door, which was possibly an escape route for those stationed there. They were still scouting for tripwires and booby traps.

On the other side of the RV, Sarge and Arvid discussed possible strategy with Kye via a video comm link. Stu could hear every word and chafed at the exile he endured.

"Stukavarius, would you like to join us?" Sarge's tone was irritatingly similar to the one his mother used to take when he had gotten up to typical boyhood mischief. Like he was in some damn time out chair.

Ignoring his brother's snickers, he moved to study the satellite image Kye had sent. The two bunker entrances were marked in red, and a dirt or gravel road winding through the mountain terrain was the only way in.

"The sun sets at 18:40. We'll take the vehicles and rendezvous here at 19:10. Team one will take the main door, team two will take the rear. Do we have any idea where Keltti is, once we're inside?"

Kye sighed from the Operations room back at the castle.

"No. There aren't any blueprints or schematics for the place. We have no idea how far underground or how spread out the place is. It could extend halfway through the damn mountain for all we know. The ground is too rocky to penetrate with infrared thermal imaging cameras, so we can't even get a headcount on who will show up to the party. Simon's second, Darrell, said it stank to high heaven of humans, Vamps and Soul Eaters."

Sarge started saying something, but Stu tuned everything out as he felt his mate's attention surge back into the mating bond.

Stu?

His knees nearly buckled in relief, and his groin tightened at the intimacy of hearing her say his name in his head. *I'm here! Are you okay?*

I'm fine. Stu could hear the smile in her thoughts.

I'm coming for you. Soon. I'm thirty minutes out—

That's not soon enough. They're coming for me as soon as the sun goes down.

Deadly rage filled his blood, heating him from the inside out and making his eyes glow red. Arvid and Ros took a step back; his face must have given away his abrupt fury. *Who? Who is coming, Sunshine?*

They called him Doc. I think he's human and works for a Vamp named Kallikan. They're experimenting on humans.

"Fuck!" Nobody jumped at his sudden outburst. His brothers continued to stand at attention, ready for whatever news Stu would impart. "They're experimenting on humans. We need to get her out of there *now.*"

They took this new intel in stride, skipping past any surprise they felt, ready to adjust their plans accordingly.

There are two Immortals with me, and I don't know how many human females. We have to get them out too. She must've sensed his hesitation, and added *Please, Stu? I can't leave them here to be lab rats.*

"There are two Immortal females, and unknown human women. We need to get them out too." There were nods of agreement all around; his brothers knew the rarity of Immortal females.

These males were members of The King's Army, the most elite army on the planet, and had taken an oath to protect not only their race, but all supernatural beings from any and all threats. The fact that there were females involved made this rescue even more important. Every male here, expect Stu, knew that there was the smallest of chances that this might be the female that they'd been waiting for to bond with.

Of course, we'll get them too.

"Can we send the Wolves in before we get there? Neutralize the threat now?" Ros suggested.

"They aren't armed." The Wolves had a fierce reputation as brawlers; most civilian Vamps would think twice before going hand-to-hand with them, but the humans were probably armed to the teeth with a variety of semi-automatic and automatic weapons. The Wolves wouldn't stand a chance in a shootout with only their fists or teeth and claws. "And we'll lose the element of surprise if we send them in now."

Stu glanced impatiently at his phone; another two hours until they could get their asses moving.

Can you find a way to barricade the door? If you can stay in the cell until I can get there—

No. There was firmness to her voice that shocked the hell out of him. *I'm not waiting around. And I'm done with you telling me what to do.*

What in God's name was she talking about? His stubborn little Witch was going to get herself killed.

Stu! Do you want to help or not? Now *she* sounded impatient.

Did he want to help with the rescue of his own mate? Fuck no! He wanted to do more than help; he wanted to be the whole damn cavalry that came to her rescue! He didn't want her to risk so much as breaking one fucking nail doing what should be his duty. But somehow, he knew that wasn't the response she was looking for. So, he gritted his teeth and tried to feint a calm that he wasn't feeling.

Yes, I'd like to help. May the Gods help him, this was not how a bonded male was supposed to act. Didn't she know how dangerous it was for her to deny him his right to protect his female? The intoxicating blend of hormones caused by the mating bond were pumping through his system, wearing away at his self control and rational thought. A bonded male denied his mate would do anything—fucking *anything*—to get her back. He was so on board with smashing some heads in. Tearing out some throats. With his fucking fangs.

Say please.

What? Did she just tell him…

Say. Please.

His brothers were going to have to get used to seeing him in his skivvies, because it was official—he no longer wore the pants in this relationship. He probably never had—he just hadn't known it until now.

Stu had argued venomously against her plan. He'd tried to guilt her into abandoning it, ordered her to forget it, begged her not to do it. He had even forbidden her from trying to escape until he was there. Big, stupid Vampire—didn't he know that women born in this century didn't take kindly to being told what to do? Forbidding a female to do something only made her want to do it that much more.

She found a small hairline crack in the floor and seated herself cross-legged with a folded blanket under her bum; the ground was cold and hard, and she would be here for a while. Placing the empty cardboard chip bowl down, she filled it with the three apple cores left over from their meal. Karina filled it with water and stepped back.

Keltti sent her a reassuring smile and gestured to the two sets of bunks. "You'll be safer under there." The two Immortals crawled under the metal beds without any argument.

"You are one crazy Witch. Is this really going to work?"

Karina's eyes were huge, the shadows turning them to a deep plum.

"It'll work." Maybe. Possibly. It had to.

Calling on her healing powers, she pulled the light from within herself and sent it down into the bowl. It swirled through the water, surrounding the apples. She guided it, targeting the tiny brown seeds that held the promise of new life. They split, tiny roots shooting out and digging past the waxy layer, into the soft paper of the bowl. Small sprouts reached up, seeking a sun that they couldn't see.

The roots consumed the soggy dish, reaching further and further as they crept across the floor. Keltti led them, showing them the small fault in the stone floor, urging them to explore as they grew. The crack widened as they burrowed down, searching for nutrients in the soil far below the rock.

Sweat beaded on her back, soaking into her shirt. The crack split with a small snapping sound, widening further and sending small sharp pieces of rock flying. She poured even more power into the new life beneath her fingertips.

She lowered her shields and reached for the connection that bound her to her mate; and a wall of worry and frustration and fear slammed into her through the mating bond. Her healing light faltered as her attention was preoccupied by Stu's chaotic emotions.

I'm okay, she tried to reassure him. *I need your help.*

Anything.

More power.

His power, strong and steady, swept through her like a summer lightning storm. Electricity heated her blood, tasting like spicy male and gunpowder. The mating bond kept her grounded, and gave her something to hold onto when she felt herself starting to drift away from the sudden surge of energy.

The small sprouts shot up, curling against the rough ceiling, seeking until they found the bare lightbulb. They delved beneath the metal socket to the copper and plastic wiring beneath. They pushed further, instinct guiding them upwards towards the waiting sun. The glass bulb shattered with a tinkle, scattering shards across the cell and plunging them into darkness.

She sent more power, her body humming with the effort of channelling so much energy at once. The sprouts thickened into saplings, twining together as they twisted upwards. Sharp shards of rock rained down as the ceiling started to crumble.

Somewhere an alarm started to blare, and the shouting of guards came closer. Her body started to shake, struggling to feed as much power into the young trees as she could. The floor shifted, and the thick glass wall fractured down the middle, small spider webs of cracks spreading outwards. Two human guards banged on the door, yelling at her with words that she tuned out. Keys jingled merrily, oblivious to the destruction around them as the guards tried to get the door open.

Tender new buds opened on the thin branches, their leaves unfurling with bright splashes of green that Keltti felt rather than saw. Upwards they went, sliding through the ever-widening crack and disappearing from sight. The crack stretched past the boundaries of the cell now, and pieces of rock and dust showered the guards.

Under all the pandemonium, she could feel her mate's reassuring presence and her heart warmed towards the bossy, chauvinistic Vampire. His desire to help her warred with his need to safeguard her from harm, and she loved him all the more for trusting her to do this.

And there it was—the one small word that she'd been afraid to give to anyone since she'd lost her mother. Something she'd subconsciously avoided sharing because life was fragile, and she didn't want her happiness dependant on someone else's existence.

But the fear and anxiety that used to dominate her thoughts of the male had faded, leaving in their place a deep conviction that he wouldn't let death steal him anytime soon. Her mate was stronger than any male she'd ever met, a deadly Warrior, who was more than capable of taking care of himself. And most importantly, he now had her to look after him. Not that he'd see it that way. Too bad for him— he was hers and she took care of what was hers. Nothing got between a Shepard and her flock.

I love you. The words felt right, and she knew she meant every one of them.

His shock rippled through their bond, immediately replaced by wonder and pure male pride. His raw honest emotions made her light headed with their intensity.

Sunshine, I… Ah…

It's okay, just show me tonight. She didn't need to hear the words—she was already aware of the emotions swirling through him.

She smiled, feeling more centered than she had in over a decade. The smell of new growth, new life, surrounded her. She pushed even more healing light into the trees, feeling the smooth bark on their trunks roughen beneath her hands.

The glass wall exploded with a *bang!* and shards of glass blasted through the air with enough force to make her ears hurt. Metal walls screeched in protest as they shifted and settled with the mountain. A few of the rivets popped free and pinged harmlessly against the opposite wall before landing on the ground.

One of the guards went down when a large rock the size of a fist landed on his head, knocking him unconscious. The other stumbled over the broken glass into the cell.

Somewhere far above, she felt the last rays of daylight kiss the new leaves she'd brought to life. They stretched, embracing their new freedom, taking their rightful place among the existing foliage.

"Stop! Don't move!" The guard held a gun, aiming straight down the barrel at Keltti's chest. "What the fuck happened in here?"

She was exhausted from using so much power, and had

no problem arranging her face into a mask of innocent confusion. "Oh, my goodness, I must've hit my head. What happened?" Her fingers tentatively probed her forehead to find one of the shallow cuts from when the light had exploded. "Oh no! I'm bleeding!"

A tinny voice squawked over his walkie talkie, sounding as agitated as the guard did, demanding an update.

"Cell three breach. I've got an injured female." So, he hadn't spotted Karina and Lysette under the bunks yet. His eyes started to sweep the destroyed room, and Keltti moaned dramatically to pull his attention back to her.

"My head! Owww…" She ignored the snort of laughter that came from the other side of the room and let her eyes flutter shut like she was going to faint.

"We need the Doc in cell three! What's the ETA?" He crept closer, but not close enough for Keltti to touch. Wise choice. He obviously knew she wasn't human.

But it didn't really matter, because once he had his back to Karina, she crawled out from under the bed and grabbed a chunk of rock the size of a softball. One quick hit to the back of his head, and he pitched forward, smacking his forehead on one of the tree trunks.

"Nice aim."

"Nice acting. Now let's get the freak out of here."

CHAPTER 19

Simon watched the last rays of sunlight disappear as dusk overtook the forest. He held out his hand, and someone handed him a cell phone. Hitting redial, his call was immediately answered by the Vampire, Kyenel.

"What do you have for me?" Kye's voice was casual, but Simon's heightened Were senses could pick up the underlying tension. He obviously cared a great deal about Keltti; all the Vamps he'd met today did. They were hell bent on getting her back and had put aside any personal dislike for Simon's kind. Except for Stu, the angry looking one— he would gladly put a knife in Simon's back without a second thought.

"I found the tree." He reached out to run his fingers over the bark of the tree, reassuring himself it was real. Once the call had come in, asking him to locate an apple tree—a fucking apple tree, in the middle of a boreal forest!—he'd assumed the Vamps were out of their fucking minds.

He'd spread the word to his Wolves, and they'd caught the fresh sweet smell in no time. It was a beauty of a tree, with multiple trunks all braided together. There should have been apples this time of year, the overripe ones littering the ground beneath the branches, but there weren't any. Magic lingered around the robust tree, faintly smelling of Keltti.

"Great, I'll let them know. They're already on their way." How in the hell was an apple tree going to lead the Vamps to the Witch? He doubted Kye would tell him; the King's Army was big on keeping things hush, hush.

"We can hear alarms, and some shouting coming from underground." He'd assumed the Vamps had attacked early, but that clearly wasn't the case.

"Yeah," Kye laughed. "That was our girl; she escaped the holding cell block and has been giving the guards a run for their money. Seriously though, keep an eye out for her. In case she manages to make it out before we can get there."

"Of course." Every Wolf in his Pack was already on high alert; finding her was their number one priority until their Alpha said differently. He had no intention of letting Kye know that Keltti's escape was already known to him. He had four Wolves stationed at each door, and their keen hearing was picking up everything that came over the guard's walkie talkies. As their Alpha, he could directly communicate with each of them to get updates.

The guards had as much chance of finding her as the Vamps did. They would both be stumbling around in the dark. He fought the urge to lead his Pack into the bunker. The Vamps considered this their fight, and he didn't want to step on any toes. Sometimes diplomacy sucked.

Stu was out of the vehicle before Vernar had even slowed to a stop. They left Gladys in the woods, half a kilometer from the main entrance, and they hiked in.

Two dark figures peeled away from the shadows beside the road; Stu's guns were unholstered and aimed at them before they could take one more step. Wet fur and animal filth—he'd know that smell anywhere. Wolves. They'd only managed to get so close without detection because the whole fucking area was permeated with their stink.

Any other night he wouldn't have lowered his weapons so quickly, but tonight his only concern was getting to his mate. The Alpha raised a single eyebrow mockingly, both knowing Stu wasn't going to shoot him. Punching him in his pretty-boy face, though… That might still be on the table if he kept looking at Stu that way…

Two Wolves whom Stu hadn't even noticed behind the

males growled, their teeth flashing in the semi-darkness.

"Easy boys, let's not forget why we're here." Simon pitched his voice low and soothing, and the Wolves quieted immediately.

Stu strode past the Shifters with Vernar and Tor close behind; he didn't even bother to turn around to see if the Wolves were with them.

The lab was something that you would see in B-list horror movies. The kind with dirty scalpels and bone-saws scattered across the counter, and a floor drain crusted with dried blood. It really shouldn't have been called a lab at all. It looked more like a torture chamber than anything that could be used for conducting research or offering first aid. The lighting was better in this room than in the corridor, and it chased away any shadows that tried to linger.

There were three padded tables in the center of the room bolted to the stone floor, all complete with leather restraints. Four small cages lined one wall, not even tall enough for a small human woman to stand up straight in. They were all empty of life, each holding only a small cot with a threadbare blanket. Two of the cage doors hung wide open, as if their occupants had left in a hurry.

Keltti quickly searched the room, verifying that there were no human women in any of the cages, while the other two females each grabbed the closest scalpel they found. The Nymph held hers tight against her chest, clutching it in a white-knuckled grip, her eyes darting nervously between the door that they had entered from and a closed one at the back of the lab.

Lysette grabbed a roll of medical tape and methodically taped scalpels to each of her forearms. Two more were taped to the skin on the sides of her calves under her black jeans. She handed Karina something that looked like a small hatchet, then turned and lifted her shirt. "Make sure I can reach the handle." Once that was taped across her shoulder blade, she stuffed a serrated saw into the back of her pants.

There were just enough sharp pairs of medical scissors to hang through each belt loop, and she kept the two largest knives in her hands.

She looked expectantly at the other women and nodded at the door.

"Right, we should keep moving." Keltti agreed, while exchanging a disbelieving look with Karina. Lysette went first this time; moving exactly like the King's Warriors when they were out in the field. How had she never noticed the female's graceful movements until now?

"They got out somehow—the human women they were holding." Karina's relief was evident and Keltti whole-heartedly agreed. It would also be easier to remain undetected without extra bodies. She just hoped they had escaped on their own to find freedom, instead of being dragged off to another location by whomever had locked them up in the first place.

The entrance wasn't much more than a hole in the rock face, set back from the road about fifteen feet. It would have been easy to overlook if not for the two human guards surveying the quiet forest, unaware that they were the ones under surveillance. The alarms from earlier had ended abruptly, leaving behind an eerie silence.

"Team two, in place." Ros's voice came over the comm link.

"Take out the guards, keep it quiet as long as you can." Sarge gave the go-ahead. Tor and Stu crept up behind the unaware guards and took them each out with a hit to the back of the head. They left the bodies where they wouldn't be seen from the road, in case any curious hikers happened to come by.

Six huge Wolves darted past the Warriors and melted into the darkness, splitting their numbers between the two corridors that led in different directions. The Captain motioned for Stu and Tor to go right, while he would go left with Simon and the other Wolf that hadn't shifted.

The stone tunnel was rough and had obviously been constructed without a lot of thought or care put into it. The ceiling was about eight feet high in most places, and bare bulbs hung from crude sockets every ten feet, alternating with deep pockets of shadow. Smaller tunnels branched off in other directions, but the Warriors kept to the main tunnel until Stu called for them to stop where one of the four-legged Wolves waited at an intersection.

"She came through here." Stu would recognize the scent of his mate anywhere—she'd passed through here recently. He felt his fangs drop when he caught the unmistakable scent of her blood. It was faint, but even one spilt drop made him want to kill whatever had caused her to bleed.

Where are you?

I don't know; these tunnels are like a hamster maze. We just passed the lab.

Gods, it felt good to hear her voice. The mating bond tightened, like a coiled rope, and he could feel her in the tunnel to the left.

I'm coming, Sunshine. Just stay where you are. He took off at a run, his heart pounding and his chest swelling with so many emotions that he couldn't even name them all. She was so damn close now; he could practically feel her soft curves in his arms already.

A gunshot echoed down the dark tunnel, and he heard his little Witch scream in fear.

The three women ducked, as a second bullet bit into ceiling above their heads, sending a shower of rock in all directions. Keltti's sandals slid on the uneven ground and she fell to her knees.

A bellow of rage and fear ripped through the air, and she didn't need the mating bond to feel her mate's panic.

"Don't shoot 'em!"

"I'm just scarin' 'em."

"Doc will be pissed if they're hurt." One of the guards grunted in acknowledgement as they continued to creep closer. There were four of them, all dressed in the typical dark shirt and pants that passed as a sort of uniform. Well-muscled and well-armed, they surrounded the three females.

"Come on ladies, it's time to go back to your nice cozy cell now." The guard leered at them, making the scar across his cheek and nose flex in a macabre kind of way. He pulled a set of zip ties from one of his cargo pockets and grabbed Karina by the arm.

"Get your hands off me, you big disgusting sac of Arnold wannabe! What happened to your face—it looks like a dog giving birth to a rat—"

The big blonde—who *did* look like a Schwarzenegger fan—backhanded the Nymph across the face. The only thing that kept her from falling backward was the jerk's hold on her arm.

Keltti gasped as the handle of a large medical instrument suddenly protruded from his left eye socket. He let go of Karina just as Lysette dragged a second knife across his throat, spraying blood in a graceful arc across the females.

"What the *fu*—" Another soldier stepped forward, but before he could raise his gun, Lysette drove the same knife straight into his abdomen and jerked it cleanly upwards. His body tumbled into a boneless heap on top of his innards, taking the knife with it.

Another guard grabbed Keltti around the waist and pulled her against his chest. His shirt smelled like cigarette smoke and fast food. He fumbled with zip ties, trying to capture her flailing arms while she struggled.

The last guard pointed a handgun at the ceiling and fired a warning shot.

"Nobody move!" he shouted.

Lysette crouched in a fighter's stance, her knees bent and shoulders back; one hand holding a wickedly sharp looking scalpel, the other effortlessly twirling the small hatchet as she inched sideways to put her body between the other female and the guard with the gun.

Little drops of spit hit the back of Keltti's neck as her

captor swore, his arms tightening like bands of steel that made it hard to breathe. She kicked backwards with her heel, connecting with the man's shin; pain ricocheted up her leg (stupid sandals!) and he didn't even seem to notice her efforts. She should have grabbed a knife from the lab. Or a pen. Or anything sharp. Even a tongue depressor would be better than nothing at this point.

Little black spots danced across her vision; she was running out of oxygen.

Her healing gift flared brightly in her chest, begging to be used. She resisted, hating what it could do. Memories from the only time she'd ever used it for something other than healing surfaced, vivid and unwelcome.

The Vampire held her, his breathing ragged and hot on the back of her neck. Her feet scrambled to grip the tile floor as he dragged her into her kitchen. He was mumbling to himself, obviously surprised that she hadn't been alone.

"Gotta go. Doc's waitin'. How the fuck am I supposed to get out?"

Her nose was less than an inch from his armpit and the combination of sweat and cheap deodorant was making her nauseous. She eyed the empty countertops and wished she had a knife block instead of keeping them in the drawer next to the silverware. Maybe if they got close enough, she'd be able to pull the drawer open and grab one.

Unfortunately, he pulled her towards the sink on the opposite side of the kitchen. He forced her against the metal basin, trapping her, as he tried to peer around her to get a look out the window. Probably looking for another way out, now that Stu was blocking the front door. He wouldn't find it in here; the back door had been bricked over when she'd had the kitchen remodeled. The only way out now was the French-doors that she'd put in the master bedroom which led out to a small patio and the rest of the back yard.

Three potted plants: an African violet, an aloe vera, and a bird's nest fern, sat on the wide sill. She grabbed the aloe vera—it was the most robust and likely to survive a traumatic event—and swung it backwards with every adrenaline-fueled ounce of strength she had. It connected with the Vampire's head, shattering on impact, and showering him with dirt and pieces of pottery. He cursed and lost his grip around her neck; she spun around to face him, the edge of the sink pressing painfully against her lower back.

Something inside her sparked, maybe her healing gift sensing the danger she was in, and her healing light broke free, like a wave breaking through floodgates that had been carefully erected to keep it contained. It smashed through her body, riding the line between pain and pleasure as it sought an outlet.

Her hands found his face and the light crashed into him, seeking, searching, digging deeper and deeper until she knew every inch of his anatomy. Her power surged, pulling and tugging at the magic within him, the magic that every life was built upon. It was thick and slippery like wet taffy, sluggish at first, then it slowly gained momentum as it gathered and collected around her light.

The Vampire realized something was wrong and tried to pull his face away from her hands. He backpedaled, banging into the corner of the counter in his haste. She moved with him, like they were trapped together in some sort of morbid dance. He shrieked, sounding like a tomcat in an alley fight.

She had no idea what she was doing, relying on pure instinct; or maybe it was just plain old-fashioned self-preservation. Whatever it was, she trusted it would keep her alive. She gave one sharp tug on her healing light and it came willingly, bringing along all the magic—his magic—as it flowed back into her body.

The Vamp's body, now devoid of what was keeping him alive, broke down piece by piece. His cells disintegrated, and his heart and major organs rotted while his brain struggled to pull any energy available into itself. His eyes, a pale sky-blue, were wide with terror, and she watched as the life in them faded.

Horror filled her at what she'd done. Yanking her hands away, the last of her healing light snapped back into her body painfully, and the now dead Vampire's head exploded with a bang! *Decomposing pieces of flesh and brain splattered her face. Thick and black, they clung to her skin and slowly ran downwards.*

"What did I do?"

Do no harm. Those words had been drilled into her from a young age. Her gift was supposed to be used for good. All Witches, regardless of what gifts they possessed, knew that.

But now, her conscience warred with her desire to live—and she wanted to live, dammit!

Her vision had gone entirely black now, and her movements were sluggish and lethargic. She could feel Stu's presence, close, but not close enough to get to her before she passed out.

Her fingertips brushed the back of her captor's hand, and her light surged into him. It wasn't kind or gentle this time; it plundered and ripped everything it could from his screaming body, feeding her the energy. The floor rushed up to catch her, and she landed next to the guard as his head exploded into an anticlimactic spurt of black oily goo. Gross.

Stu rounded a corner in the tunnel, guns drawn as the scent of blood got stronger. His body vibrated with the need to find her. She was close. So fucking close…

A tangle of bodies lay motionless in a large puddle of bodily fluids. Past that, a small female crouched in a defensive stance, holding a hatchet and a handgun. She leveled it at his chest with a hand covered in blood. Her dark hair and clothing blended in with the blood and black goo that stained her arms and face.

He kept both his gun's trained on her while he calmly regarded the rest of the gory scene. Behind her, another female with long white hair watched him warily with large violet eyes. Pain and defiance covered her delicate features. Next to her, someone kneeled… his mate!

She looked up, green eyes shining in the dim lighting, and he felt his heart stop for a moment before redlining it in his suddenly tight chest. Her small cry of joy just about undid him, and he barely had time to holster his guns before she launched herself over the dead bodies and into his arms.

"I knew you'd come." Tears ran down her dirty face, leaving tiny tracks in the filth. Gods, she had never looked more beautiful. He ran his hands over her, trying to reassure himself she was unharmed. The mating mark on her neck hummed with recognition when he stroked his fingers over it. Finally satisfied that she was in one piece, he tugged her into a desperate kiss that left them both breathless.

Behind him, Tor cleared his throat and gestured to the small female still pointing a gun in their direction.

"Lysette, it's okay. They're here to help." His mate used the same soothing tones one would use when talking to an injured child. The gun lowered, but the distrustful look stayed on her face.

Somewhere off in the distance an explosion rumbled; the ground beneath them started to shake, and the lights flickered several times before deciding to stay on. One of the Shifters, still in Wolf form, whined.

"Time to move!" Sarge ordered.

The Warriors quickly herded the females back the way they'd come. Stu kept his arm protectively around his Witch the entire time, not willing to risk losing her again. The Wolves loped ahead, and Tor dropped back to guard their asses as they tried to find their way out of the underground maze.

CHAPTER 20

Kallikan sat in a pool of blood. It had long ago soaked into his fatigues, solidifying into a gelatinous mess that had no doubt cemented his boxers to the short curlies on his backside. It would probably hurt like a son of a bitch when he had to rip them off. Not that he cared. His thoughts were only for the female in his arms.

Her long golden hair hid under layers of dirt and blood, tangled from her thrashing against the pillows. Her sightless eyes, once the color of the calmest ocean, were now greyed in death. Bruises covered her wrists and ankles; he'd had to restrain her from hurting herself. The pale purple nightgown was surprisingly clean—most of her blood had spilt on the sheets.

"*Sarafeena…*" His whispered plea went unanswered. Again.

The dead didn't talk. He'd heard rumors that some supernaturals could hear them. Maybe if he'd found one of them sooner… No, it didn't matter now. She was gone.

Such piss poor timing too. He'd finally found the healing Witch that he'd been hunting. The human Doctor he'd been working with, Dr. Liphspen, had been certain the Witch could help Sara.

A tear landed on her face, and Kallikan hollowly realized it was his. He hadn't known he was still capable of crying. He tried to give a shit at the revelation. Nope, he didn't have it in him. His give-a-fuck must be broken. Right along with the body cradled in his arms.

The sound of gunshots reached him, muffled by the walls of his personal chamber. They wouldn't find him in here; the door was well hidden, its location known only to himself now that Sara was gone.

Voices rose and fell as they passed by his room unaware. Let them go. Keeping the females was pointless now. They didn't deserve the same fate as his Sara. He felt the presence of other Vampires—the King's Warriors were here. The potency of their bloodlines made them easy to sense.

And Shifters. A lot of Shifters. That was vaguely interesting; the two didn't usually mix well together. Either way, he knew the females would be safe.

The dresser across the room held fresh sheets. He would use them to wrap the dead female in, until he could find a place to bury her. If he had more time, he would have liked to clean her head wound, and maybe wash her hair. She had always been especially diligent about things like grooming, even before modern conveniences like indoor plumbing had come along. He'd helped her with the task of combing out the tangles more than once.

Nights spent next to the fire with his hands full of her silky tresses had been replaced by pain and madness and guilt and bone-deep sorrow.

And blood.

So much damn blood.

"Team two report!" Sarge continued, trying to reach the other Vamps on the comm link without success.

They turned a corner and found themselves in a large room that was serving as a theater. A large white projection screen took up nearly an entire wall. Large speakers sat in each corner, and a variety of colored couches from different eras sat facing the screen. Apparently, they'd found the break room.

Bullets filled the air as a large group of human guards entered the area from a separate tunnel. One of the females screamed, and the Warriors pushed them behind the safety of an overturned table.

The brothers returned fire, careful to keep track of the Shifters so that they wouldn't be caught in the crossfire. Two of the guards went down from gunshots, and another screamed as one of Lysette's scalpels was thrown across the room, lodging directly in his chest.

One of the Wolves slipped around the couches, his dark brown fur blending into the shadows, until he was close enough to tackle one of the guards. The sounds of cartilage crunching and muscles tearing filled the air, as he ripped out the man's throat.

The guards closest to the tunnel suddenly dropped, taking fire from the direction they'd just come from. Stu waited until their attention was divided, and then started picking them off one by one. The other Wolves moved in to attack anyone who was stupid enough to expose their back.

Once the last guard had fallen, Arvid glided out of the far tunnel, followed by Ros, Adrian, Simon, and another male Shifter. Half a dozen Wolves followed, flowing like water around the bodies as they circled the room. A few stopped and nuzzled Keltti's face until a foul look from Stu had them slinking away.

"We need Keltti!" Ros called, even as she was running across the room to get to where Adrian was sitting against the wall. Blood soaked the right leg of his pants, and he clutched his leg above the knee to try to stop the flow. Sweat stood out on his pale face, his features pinched into a grimace.

It was a hell of an initiation; every Warrior could recall their first combat situation, and Adrian would have a hell of a story to tell after tonight. Staking a claim in this war came at a cost—one that he'd just paid for in blood and pain. The male was a true Warrior now, and Stu was surprised to find himself smiling. About fucking time. Later they'd welcome him into the brotherhood with a blood ceremony, once everyone was safely out of this hell hole.

"Mother *fucker!* Fuck, that hurts! Shit-on-a-stick-" he broke off when Keltti knelt next to him, giving him one of her reassuring smiles. "Sorry, Keltti—"

"Its okay, I know it hurts." Gods, his mate was so patient with the male; he was just so damn proud of her. "Try to relax, I'm just going to take a peek." She closed her eyes, and Stu could feel her power echoing though his own body as she worked her magic.

Nobody spoke. Every one of the Warriors was still awed when they bore witness to her talent. Reverence and gratitude shone in their eyes, along with a few haunted looks from those who had escaped death because of this female. *His* female. Yeah, *so* damn proud.

"There, that should get you on your feet long enough to make it home." She held up the bullet that had fallen on the floor and scrunched up her nose. "It's just a regular bullet; no poison."

Stu bent and confiscated a gun from the nearest body. He ejected the magazine and slid the first few bullets into his hand. "She's right, these are only regular, lead, hollow point rounds. It would take a hell of a lot of these to kill one of us."

"So, they weren't trying to kill us?" Arvid asked.

"Who knows. They're human, maybe they don't know what they're up against." Ros shrugged indifferently.

"Can I keep the bullet?" Adrian asked. Keltti handed him the bullet and he hastily added, "For Ollie. He'll think it's cool."

Arvid helped Adrian to his feet, and Sarge ordered everyone down the tunnel from which team two had come. Stu clung to Keltti's side like a fucking wet blanket—she wouldn't be safe until they were out of this underground pit.

Karina shrieked when one of the guards at her feet suddenly moved, his movements sluggish and uncoordinated as he jerked something out of his pocket and threw it across the room.

"Grenade!"

There was a flurry of movement as everyone dove for cover. Stu swung Keltti off of her feet and ran for the tunnel. Tor had been in the rear and ran forward, slamming into Karina to send her flying across the room towards the exit.

The grenade exploded, filling the room with a roar as it unleashed its power, blinding and deafening anyone in its path as it tore through the mountain. The ceiling heaved, sending rock blasting apart as clouds of dust burst into the air, making it hard to breathe. Stu covered his mate, shielding her with his body as debris pummelled them. Every time he thought it was over, the Earth shuddered and made one more attempt to bury them alive.

Grunts of pain and coughing became more noticeable as Stu's hearing started to clear. His mate struggled to move, trying to get out from under his bulk; she could probably hear the injured and wanted to get to them. Not until he thought it was safe.

"Not yet," he whispered into her hair. The pitter patter of tiny pebbles falling from the ceiling still continued as the mountain shifted, trying to find its final resting position. He let his weight settle over hers, felt her curves accept his hardness willingly. Taking several deep breaths, he filled himself with the scent of his mate. He clenched his fists, trying to ward off the trembling that was starting. Gods, his mate had nearly died. Again. What the fuck was wrong with this world that it kept throwing this shit at her?

He was going to tie her to his bed, and never let her leave. Nothing could hurt her there. He'd have to get more locks for the door. Actually, he could install a vault door like the banks had—

Stop! I'm fine. Her small hands delved under his shirt so she could caress the skin on his back. She'd quit squirming to get free and wiggled her hips until they were cradling his. Oh shit, had she been reading his thoughts?

Stu? Let's go home.

Yeah, they should go. Definitely go. His brothers could

be hurt; they'd probably need her help. He should get up. But his stupid body didn't care about anything but the feel of her beneath him. And his idiot cock—*dumb-ass, selfish little bastard!*—was in total agreement, hardening against the apex of her legs while he silently cursed at himself.

This mating was going to be the death of him. If she didn't kill him first.

Nothing had linked the underground bunker to the Rebels, which didn't sit well with Arvid. They had been quiet for too long; the bastards were definitely up to something.

This also raised the question of who had been behind the fucked-up chamber of horrors? The only thing they had to go on were rumors of the mysterious Kallikan. There was lots of supposition regarding the possibility of genetic experiments on Immortals and humans alike, but no actual proof.

There was also the baffling visit from Calder Courtland and his outlandish claims of an American Government Organization kidnapping and exploiting Psionics, just two days after Keltti and Stu's recuse by the mystifying Hadley. Who may or may not be human. Or Psionic. If such a breed of supernatural really existed.

It all added up to a big heaping load of fuck-all.

And then, there was the female laying on the bed in front of him. She'd been here in the infirmary hooked to an IV since he found her at the abandoned house. Daily visits from Keltti had upgraded her status from a mummified corpse to a shriveled body with barely a heartbeat.

Ommi had even started spending time reading to her. The two of them made quite a sight—two beautiful females, their bodies aged beyond anything a Vampire should ever be capable of. Yet, here they were, two amazing marvels of nature; one aging further everyday, while the other slowly struggled to turn back the hands of time.

Keltti was calling her sleeping state a "hibernation of the soul."

Her long red hair had fallen out, and soft stubble was starting to cover her pale scalp. And yeah, Arvid knew firsthand just how soft it really was. Laying hands on a helpless female was so far beneath a Warrior of his station, but he was a fucking selfish bastard and didn't regret it in the least.

Her skin had softened around her bones, losing the papery texture. It looked as though it was one spa-day away from normal. He wondered what color her eyes were. Something vivid he'd bet.

In human years, she looked to be about four hundred. But she wasn't human. The undeniable spark of magic inside him that recognized others of his kind identified her as a Vampire. A *female* Vampire.

He knew the other Warriors often checked in on her. He didn't blame them; it had been so long since any of them had spent time around an unmated female. They had contact with regular citizens, but the Warriors' presence raised the protective instincts of every father with an unmated daughter. Just the sight of the males on patrol had them locking the females of their race away in hidden rooms. Unmated or not.

Seeing Stu find his life mate had hit them all hard, driving home the fact that they didn't stand a chance in hell of finding their own. And then fate had gone and dropped this lovely female right at their doorstep—unchaperoned and unmated.

After dressing her in a simple hospital gown, Keltti had assured them there was no mating mark present.

Not that it was any of his business. But a male could dream, right?

EPILOGUE

Stu's bedroom had five new residents; and he had welcomed them all.

The first was his little Witch. He'd insisted she move into Bloddrikker Castle until he could take care of all the security concerns he had with her bungalow. And if he never totally satisfied those concerns... Well, then she'd just have to stay here with him indefinitely.

The other new occupants had shown up over the last few weeks, appearing randomly when he wasn't looking. The first was a small pointy-leafed thing in a yellow pot that made itself at home on his dresser. The second and third were taller, with wide round leaves that fluttered happily whenever his mate walked past. His last new adoptee hung from the ceiling in a white basket next to the window, its long skinny vines already latched onto the curtain rod, wrapping themselves stubbornly in place. The little pine tree Stu had dug up for Keltti had even moved in, heartily enjoying a new ceramic pot in the castle lobby as it stood watch over the main doors.

Stu had tried to tell her they wouldn't be happy here with the shutters closed all day, but they were tough like his little Witch and making themselves right at home.

The irony wasn't lost on him; the way she'd taken him, a hopeless creature of the dark, and brought him back into the light, healing parts of him he hadn't even known were broken. Figuratively of course, because he was still a Vamp and would literally fry in the sun. But he could live without that shit. And he had something even better now. His *mate*.

His Sunshine. And a big ass smile on his face. Who'd have thought?

A handful of sheer scarves were draped over the mirror; the blues, greens, yellows, and peaches added colour to his otherwise plain room. The gun cabinet sat across from the mirror; he'd moved it out of the closet to make room for some of Keltti's things. Every week, more of her long skirts and soft sweaters appeared next to his fighting leathers and workout sweats. He was especially looking forward to when the snow would disappear, because she'd start wearing those feminine little sundresses again.

Although, when the nights were especially cold, she'd snuggle extra close so he could warm her with his body heat. Maybe winter could stick around a bit longer. Or maybe he'd just turn the thermostat down a few degrees before bed…

He wasn't surprised when the door burst open and slammed into the wall. He'd felt her presence as she'd gotten closer, her excitement humming pure and golden through their bond. Her green eyes were incandescent in the dark bedroom, and they met his with a smile that lit up his whole body. His whole damn world, actually.

"They found him!" She waited expectantly as his eyes traveled leisurely over her body, lingering on the delicious curves that made her so incredibly female.

"Stu…"

He licked his lips; the pale lace of her bra was peeking out of her shirt. He knew the exact sound she'd make if he went over there and sucked on her rosy nipples through the fabric.

"Stu!" She gestured towards her face. "Eyes up here, big guy!"

He smiled, knowing there was nothing even remotely apologetic about it. The impatient look she gave him was worth it.

"They found Tor." He sat up, his body suddenly tense as he waited for her to continue. "He's alive."

"Oh, Gods… He's alive." His lungs remembered how to work again, and he pulled in a huge breath. His little Witch climbed onto the bed next to him, wrapping her arms around his neck.

"They'll be here soon with him; I have to go." Of course, she did; he'd go with her.

Tor had been buried under the mountain of rock two months ago when the grenade had gone off. Everyone had been working relentlessly to find him. Several civilian Vamps had come forward with their knowledge and skills in the excavation field. Even the Dark Shadow Pack was helping with the grunt labour.

"How bad is he?" A Vamp could survive a hell of a lot, but without food or blood, he wouldn't be able to heal.

"I don't know. Kye wouldn't tell me anything."

It was probably pretty bad if Kye hadn't been forthcoming with the details. Keltti's worry was leaking through their bond, sending little spikes of pain through his chest. He didn't bother trying to downplay the situation with empty words; they both knew her fears were well founded.

He leaned down and pressed his lips to hers, needing to chase the apprehension from her face. She softened against him, her body swiftly growing pliant in his arms as he deepened the kiss.

"How long until they get here?" He murmured against her full lips.

"Twenty minutes?" she guessed, while her hands ran across his bare chest.

It would take three minutes to get downstairs, or only two if they ran. That left eighteen minutes to kill until she was needed…

He was more than happy to help her pass the time.

~

ABOUT THE AUTHOR

Born and raised on the beautiful Canadian prairies, Everlyn prefers to spend her time outdoors with her family kayaking, skating, fishing, and hunting.

She loves reading and writing about vampires, witches, fae and zombies that get to find their own version of happily ever after.

Find out more about Everlyn and her books at:

WWW.EVERLYNCTHOMPSON.COM

Other Vampire Novels by Burton Mayers Books:

Fiona's Guardians – *Dan Klefstad*

October's Son aka The London Vampire &

Nuptial Flight – *John Michaelson*

CPSIA information can be obtained
at www.ICGtesting.com
Printed in the USA
BVHW032255170223
658757BV00002B/65

9 781739 630973